LUCKY YOU

LUCKY YOU

A NOVEL

ERIKA CARTER

COUNTERPOINT
BERKELEY

Library of Congress Cataloging-in-Publication Data is available.

Cover design by Kelly Winton
Interior design by Sabrina Plomitallo-González

ISBN 978-1-61902-899-9

COUNTERPOINT
2560 Ninth Street, Suite 318
Berkeley, CA 94710
www.counterpointpress.com

Printed in the United States of America
Distributed by Publishers Group West

10 9 8 7 6 5 4 3 2 1

FOR ROB

CONTENTS

LUCKY YOU

SUSTAINABILITY

ELLIE

An ice storm just knocked the electricity out, like the weatherman said it would—but did she listen? She didn't listen. She didn't prepare. She had flashlights with dead batteries, candles but no matches. A fireplace full of plants.

The TV had been on all week, and the apartment's new silence filled her with what was not quite loneliness, but the fear of loneliness—as though if she were fast, she could stop it altogether, and a beat of panic set her going.

She did that—kept the TV on—every time her boyfriend stayed gone playing music in Texas bars. She knew all the morning talk-show queens, the vicious and beautiful of daytime, the sitcoms. She paced the floors reading haikus against the laugh tracks. At night it was preachers preaching in megachurches, faded movie stars selling jewelry.

Jim took his banjo and stomp box and harmonicas and all three of his shirts to Austin. For he didn't know how long, he said. Probably a week, he said. Except it had been over a week now. The last thing he said before he drove away was, "Don't be sad."

But the cat lay over the vent where heat normally fired out, and that made her sad. And she *was* sad, she was always sad when he was gone, and it was around this time—the week marker—that she started getting into trouble.

The last light had drained behind the buildings when she crossed the street and passed a frozen bed of pansies, little yellow screams, to enter the neon-dark of Viceroy.

Smoke misted over the pool table. The chain of booths sat empty, but a few men sat at the bar, watching the sports channel and its ribbon of scores across the bottom. Two-dollar drafts until seven.

She worked here, so she drank for free when Bruce and Lorraine turned their heads. What she needed was to talk to

Chloe. Chloe the listener. Chloe let her talk about herself, let her get it all out.

But she could *not* stay out late, she told herself. She could not stay until two. Part of her knew she would, and it made her sad knowing she couldn't trust herself.

Chloe poured her a generous Jameson in a tumbler. Bruce was already gone, Chloe told her, afraid of tonight's black ice. He'd also had another fight with Lorraine, who was in the kitchen mixing tomorrow's Fresh Lobster Bisque.

The Fresh Lobster Bisque was into its third reheat of the week, and who knew where the lobster *came* from. This was Arkansas.

At eleven, she was admitting that she hadn't heard from Jim all week. "He doesn't call me," Ellie said.

Chloe's lack of response almost had a calming effect. Maybe this was why Chloe was so easy to talk to, Ellie thought. Or was it, she thought, because Chloe was sort of a little ugly? For one thing, she was going bald. Patches of pale scalp spotted through the crown of her barrettes. She was very thin, and since she'd gone vegan her skin had become weirdly clear—you could see the channels of little blue veins in her cheeks and on her eyelids.

Ellie had met Jim at Natalie's Majestic Lounge near the end of summer. She came one afternoon with Rachel and stayed until two. But she'd eaten lunch, at least, and in the bathroom mirror above the cracked sink, her eyes still looked normal—focused and wide and not too watery.

That had been just before Rachel quit Viceroy and moved with her boyfriend to a little house deep in the Ozark Mountains. "We are in the midst of a large-scale ecological crisis,"

Rachel kept insisting. She was reading a book called *Toward Sustainability* and occasionally she would retrieve it from her purse and read passages out loud.

Ellie had nodded in agreement, but she was playing eye contact with the lead singer, her chest keeping time with heat and gin and excitement. He wore a trucker hat and rolled-up Levi's and sang country songs, and she walked right up to him after his set. His name was Jim—and she'd always wanted to be with a Jim—and they flirted while she bought the album, *8-Track Motel*.

He bought her a black and tan, then followed her to her booth, where they sat thigh to thigh across from Rachel, who was talking about the bottled-water phenomenon. Consumption, overpopulation, and excess packaging were among Rachel's favorite topics.

He bought Ellie another beer and relaxed an electric hand on her thigh. Now they lived together, and he toured around Austin and Marshall and Shreveport, Louisiana. Even Little Rock. There was no point playing Fayetteville, he said, unless you were playing Natalie's—and he was sick of Natalie's. And if you were up here, he said, you may as well play Eureka Springs and Saint Louis, and he had some exes to avoid that way.

"Why don't you start going with him?" Chloe asked. Sometimes he traveled by himself, and sometimes he played with his band, Crush Heat Burn.

"No—I mean, it's his work."

"What if he's just using you for a place to live?"

Chloe was a bitch sometimes. Ellie swallowed a sip of Jameson and said, "Then why not live with a girl in Austin, where he really wants to be? Anyway, I did go with him once. This fall. To a music festival." She pushed the empty glass back toward Chloe, the sign for another. "I am not a person who goes to music festivals."

Harvest Fest '07 was on Mulberry Mountain, in Ozark. She remembered being drunk the whole time, and still bored, as she watched, from the roof of his maroon van, people wandering around on acid, people passed out on patchwork quilts, their backs getting sunburned. She remembered sitting in a circle with other people, under some trees, eating mushrooms that made her laugh, then cry.

He played a solo set on a stage in the woods, and she remembered the Hula-Hoopers revolving in front of him with their blinking neon waists. She remembered his good friend and sometimes bandmate, Phoenix, saying, "You don't belong here."

When her mother said this kind of thing, she hated her. But when Phoenix said it, she kind of loved him.

"I'm getting tired of it all," Phoenix said. "Bars, festivals, being broke all the time." He'd been wearing his red cowboy boots for the whole four-day festival, with his mane of blond hair pushed behind a beaded headband. They stood there watching Jim wet the harmonica and tap the stomp-box. "Look at Jim though, he loves it. He could do this forever."

Everyone thought Phoenix was gay, probably. She felt vaguely relieved. But for that moment at Harvest Fest, she pretended he wasn't, and she saw their future spread out—a little house with a porch swing, and animals in the yard, bikes leaned against a tree, and quiet air.

Now Chloe was yelling last call.

When had it happened, Ellie wondered, when had it become crowded? Women with fake winter tans flirted against men in sweatshirts with razorback heads all over them. Empty glasses of beer sat on the tall circular bar tables and on the edges of the pool table. She watched a man in red faded flannel chalk his cue, then strike the eight ball into the waiting pocket. She felt something when he did that, but she didn't know what it meant.

Lorraine was cruising the booths now, encouraging people to come in for brunch, to try the Fresh Lobster Bisque, to drink to the ice storm.

Ellie panicked, thinking of the iciness of the bed sheets, the cat shivering over the vent, clothes on the floor. She drank another Jameson.

After she put her coat on and weaved her fingers through the buttons, she tipped Chloe for everything she wasn't charged, then left the bar and walked down the street toward home. Cold air went through the knees of her jeans as she passed the just-closed bars that people stood outside of, busy with their phones, their faces lit up by screens like blue flames. They were entering numbers and making plans, going home with each other.

She checked her phone again. Nothing.

She turned the corner. Now there were footsteps behind her. "Hey, girl," a man's voice said. He found her stride on the sidewalk. "Where you headed?"

They turned the corner together.

"Where you headed?" he repeated.

There was a certain charm in his voice, or she imagined it, as she turned and faced him. He was tall, black, good-looking. His fists stayed in the pockets of his zipped parka.

"Home," she said. She kept walking, but she already knew something was going to happen.

"Let's hang."

She laughed and shook her head, like of course it was out of the question. And why, why couldn't she be a normal person who *would* think it was out of the question?

"Where do you live, what's your name?"

She turned around again, unable to decide whether or not to lie.

He caught her mood, and said, "Come on, be real."

She laughed nervously.

"Let me walk you home," he said, then signaled behind him. Now there were three of them. But they looked nice enough, all of them smiling at her, then back to each other.

"I don't have any power," she said, in the spirit of protest, but it came out like an apology.

"That's okay, it's cool."

She'd have one drink with them. One drink, she thought.

They walked over the bridge, the lanes glazed in black ice as though the night had been crushed. She looked over the railing at the train tracks below, and thought of the now-infamous drunk kid, an undergraduate who passed out there, one arm thrown over the steel, and the morning train that took his hand.

When she'd told Jim about this one afternoon in October, walking across the bridge with their shade-grown coffees, he put his arm around her and said, "They say during a heavy rainstorm you can see the hand, soaked in blood, slowly, *slowly* crawl back over the tracks"—which is when he squeezed her, scaring her into laughter.

The first guy was holding on to her elbow now. Even so, she almost slipped. They talked about new bars in town where they'd been drinking earlier. They knew each other from college, but not here. They talked about scones. All the random sentences in the wide net of a long night's end.

They crossed to her street where car hoods faced out of driveways and glistened at curbs, the way they were supposed to, away from the trees that looked stuck in Krazy Glue. Her neighbors, they listened. They prepared.

They were probably among the crush of shoppers at the grocery store yesterday, leaving the shelves blank when she wandered in, unable to decide what she wanted for dinner or why the commotion until she remembered about the ice storm.

At least she didn't have anywhere to go, so if she woke up to a branch through her windshield, it wouldn't really matter.

A yellow porch light burned at the end of her lane. Power. She unlocked the door and stepped into her apartment's new heat. The clocks blinked. She felt for the light switch, and they followed her inside. "Sit down," she said, gesturing to the sofa.

She put on music—a viper jazz band Jim introduced her to. She went to the kitchen and returned with the Hornitos and ceramic shot glasses. "We're taking shots," she said.

They threw them back. One guy, the first guy, asked if it was okay to light the joint he was holding in his pocket.

She said sure, but kept passing her turns. Drug tests at work, she explained, but really, she just didn't like it. The only thing she ever wanted to do when she was drinking was keep drinking.

She sat lotus-style on the floor, in front of the sofa where they sat in a row. She asked if they had wives or girlfriends. They said no. "My boyfriend doesn't want to have sex with me," she said.

"Really? Does he come onto you?" Blue gum flashed against his teeth as he talked.

"No, he comes inside of me."

"Damn! That's not what I meant—" They erupted with laughter. "No, I mean—I mean—does he—" They started laughing again. Nobody could get the sentence out.

"Listen to this. So, once he was like, 'Do you want kids?' And I go, 'I want yours.' And he just smiled. So—what does that mean? Like nothing was decided, do you see what I mean? That's how we are, like everything is one huge mis-understanding."

She could tell from their faces they weren't following. What did she just say, anyway? As soon as the words floated from her mouth, they were gone—they disappeared. Someone came back from the bathroom and bent over the lamplight of the computer to change the music. "No!" she shrieked.

"Leave it on, man. Don't be crazy."

"Wait," she said. "I thought there were four of you." She did, she honestly thought so. Who *were* these guys?

"You're fucked up, girl." The three of them introduced themselves again, but she couldn't hold on to their names.

"Do you wish there were four of us? How old are you?"

She considered lying, but found no good reason to. "Twenty-three."

So were they, they said. Her eyes passed over their faces again.

For some reason she needed them to think that she was innocent now, that this was special. "I've only slept with two people in my life," she lied. "My boyfriend in college and my boyfriend now."

"For real?"

Suddenly, she had an idea. She stood up and walked to the corner bookshelf. She reached down *The Essential Haiku: Versions of Bashō, Buson & Issa*. She had to buy the book for an English class in college, and she rediscovered it last week. She read it in the evenings, pacing the floors.

"I'm going to read you some haikus now," she said, standing in front of them. "We need to take another shot first."

"I'm shitfaced, girl."

She slammed hers back and looked into the mirror oval over the bookcase, barely able to believe how drunk she looked. Her eyes were tiny, watery slits. She looked back at them. "Just do it. Let's just get really drunk."

She had another idea: She would quit drinking forever tomorrow, which meant she should drink everything she could tonight.

"Read us the poem."

"Okay, you have to really listen. I want you to really listen."

"We're listening."

She began. "They don't live long / but you'd never know it— / the cicada's cry." She turned the page and stared at them.

They nudged each other until one of them said, "Okay. I like that."

She continued. "Even in Kyoto / hearing the cuckoo's cry / I long for Kyoto."

She looked up and turned the page. Tears stung the back of her eyes.

"Not this human sadness, / cuckoo, / but your solitary cry."

She took in their canceled expressions.

"Another shot," she said, then dropped the book on the table, harder than she meant to.

She woke up beside the condoms. Thank god they used condoms. Her stuffed animals stared back at her—the dog with the one eye—while the morning train cried through her.

She walked to the bathroom and balanced her hands on the cold sink. She looked at her body, a stranger's body. The room was everywhere; she could not escape the room. She wrapped a quilt around her like a coat, then fell back asleep to the voices discussing the healthcare crisis on *Good Morning America*. They brought in experts, they brought in congressmen, they brought in doctors.

When she woke up again, she felt a little better, but what the fuck was *wrong* with her? She could have been flung off a bridge last night. Anything could have happened, and nobody would have known.

She let the cat inside, then confronted the living room. A shot glass lay broken in several pieces on the floor. The other glasses, tequila candied at the bottoms, were lined along the table where the varnish was sticky. She wanted to laugh at the whole thing, to make herself feel better, but it was too confusing.

She carried the glasses to the sink. Icicles hung outside the window. She stared through them into her neighbor's yard—a wicker reindeer left from Christmas, its head wired out of shape. A manger scene, with a plastic Virgin staring into an empty crib.

She opened the refrigerator, but there was only the bright hum of electricity. The only cure for this unbearable hangover regret-depression was a Bloody Mary. Before she did anything, she needed to wash down breakfast with a Bloody Mary.

This was how she was fired from her last job, at the printer-supply company. She never told anyone. Because her boss was a little in love with her, he helped her find another one— administrative work for a man named Michael Lindsey, a Walmart executive. But waitressing was easier, so she'd started working at Viceroy instead. At Viceroy, she could wear jeans and drink. She'd pour herself shots of Rumple Minze and Jameson and Fireball into a coffee mug all night. If someone ordered a mimosa, she'd empty the champagne bottle into a Styrofoam cup with a lid and drink it through a straw. She'd nurse it through her shift.

Plus, Rachel and Chloe already worked there. "The money is decent," Rachel had said, persuading her. "Even if it's gross." The kitchen did do some questionable things with food, and nobody cleaned. Broken glass glittered under the booths.

After graduating from the University of Arkansas, Ellie and Rachel discovered that degrees in English, as it turned out, really were worthless. "I see now that nobody cares that I never understood *Beowulf*," Rachel said. Chloe had dropped out twelve credits shy of a degree in biology.

Now Ellie forced herself to stand up in the shower. She washed her hair and squinted at the purity of a bar of soap.

The café was back over the bridge, still slick with ice. She glanced over the train tracks, and thought of the hand separated from the body.

She found a table in the back, where the waitress's mauve lipstick wanted her order—eggs and a Bloody Mary. Fiddle music ached from the speakers in the ceiling while she tore a napkin into shreds, thinking.

Then she saw Phoenix's wave of blond hair, shorter than it was at Harvest Fest. He was paying for coffee to go, wearing his books in a canvas backpack. Why was Fayetteville like this—you always saw someone you knew just when you really didn't want to. She watched him move through the espresso line.

She went back and forth pretending not to see him—she couldn't decide—and then it was too late. He stopped at her table on his way out, doing a little double take, saying, "Ellie?"

"Oh," she said, feigning slight surprise. "Hey." She wished she'd worn makeup or something else and not the gray sweater.

"Woah. I haven't seen you since what—Harvest? Crazy. How are you? Can I sit down a minute?"

"Sure." She stood up halfway, and they hugged awkwardly. She asked how he'd been.

"Good—great, actually. I'm getting my master's in

mechanical engineering now. I start this semester." He tugged the strap of his backpack, and made a face. She forced herself to smile. He told her he quit music. "The lifestyle just isn't sustainable," he said.

"That's great," she replied, then wondered what she meant.

He looked at her Bloody Mary. "I get a headache if I drink this early," he said.

She shrugged. "I get one if I don't."

His phone rang. When he retrieved it from his pocket and looked at the screen, he said, "I have to take this." He hesitated. "It's my mom. But we should seriously catch up, yeah?"

She nodded.

"Tonight?"

Knowing she would see Phoenix made her quit after three Bloody Marys. She nursed her hangover with a pillow between her legs and the sound of TV. The mix of panic and regret and alcohol tilted against her all afternoon.

After *Everybody Loves Raymond*, a wretched, absolutely wretched show, she made the bed and folded the quilt into quarters. A wad of blue gum surprised her under the nightstand.

She remembered to charge her phone, but couldn't find the charger. She was confused because the white cord always stayed in the wall by her bookcase. Would they have stolen that, of all things? Alarmed, she tore through her purse.

She took a deep breath when she found everything— phone, wallet, keys. Her computer was on her desk, thank god. *Don't be a racist*, she told herself. She plugged the phone into her computer, in case Jim called.

But he didn't call.

Phoenix was waiting on a bench in front of Viceroy, reading the *Free Weekly*. He wore skinny jeans and his red cowboy boots and a grandfatherly yellow cardigan. They walked inside and he went to the bar for their drinks.

Chloe served him, then proceeded to stare, with her usual bored expression. Only her eyes were saying, okay, now who is *this* guy?

They talked about the election. Fayetteville was alive for Obama. "You're registered to vote, right?" Phoenix said.

"Of course." Only, she wasn't registered to vote. "You?"

"Yeah, of course. I mean, I *will* be, obviously. As long as he gets the nomination instead of Hillary."

She liked Hillary better, but you just couldn't say this kind of thing in a bar in Fayetteville. She couldn't stop tapping her foot under the table. The bar kept reminding her of last night.

"Phoenix, do you want to just go back to my apartment and get really drunk and read haikus?"

He smiled. "That sounds sublime."

"We have to go to the liquor store first."

He opened the door for her on the way out. The sidewalk dragged with shadows under the streetlights, the long forms moving in and out of doorways.

They stared at the shelves of liquor and fluorescent coolers. When Phoenix asked what she wanted, she said, "Anything." Anything, she thought, but tequila.

"What do you like?"

"You choose." Because everything, she liked everything, unfortunately.

He went to the shelf and picked out a bottle of vodka. She got the orange juice, and they walked back to her house in relative silence. She realized she was already bored. This boredom: Was this why she drank so much?

They talked facing each other on the sofa, while the cat stalked the turned-up corner of the rug, then weaved between Pheonix's red cowboy boots.

They drank steadily off coasters that read I AM NOT A FRISBEE. These were from Viceroy, where the I AM NOT A FRISBEE part made people fling them.

Phoenix was slurring, but she felt tired instead of drunk. "I thought haikus were for like, Asian people," he said, coming back from the bathroom to sit down again, closer to her, her mouthwash on his breath.

"Read me another one," he said.

"Okay." She yawned. "Coolness / the sound of the bell / as it leaves the bell." She turned the page. "Plums in blossom / and the geishas who can't go out / are buying sashes."

"I like that one," he said. He brushed a strand of hair behind his ear and transferred the book to his lap. "I really like that one." He turned the page. "The beginning of art— / a rice planting song / in the backcountry."

She didn't like the way he read. He read pretentiously.

He looked at her, then kissed her ear. She turned. "What? Wait. I thought, I thought you were"—she was afraid, somehow, of offending him—"I don't know, with someone, or something."

ERIKA CARTER · 18

"Why would you think that?"

"I mean . . . you know that Jim and I are still together, right?" She looked around the apartment, as if to show him the evidence, but looking at it this way, she realized it was mostly *her* stuff from wall to wall, that it barely looked like anyone else lived here.

"Well, I was under the impression that he crashed with you when he needed a place, but was—well, I thought he was basically living in Austin now."

"No," she said. "No. No. No."

"Are you sure?"

"What?"

"Sorry, I don't know."

She closed her eyes. "No—look, I'm sorry, I'm really tired."

Long, awkward pauses—she hated them.

"Yeah, so I'm pretty tired," she said again.

She walked him to the door, as if she were sixteen on some kind of strange date-gone-wrong at her parents' house.

He rubbed her arms while she played with the lock. After a deadly silence he said, "Good night, Ellie." She slid the chain across the door behind him.

She closed her eyes to the women selling jewelry on TV. *Real Mediterranean-inspired earrings, the bracelet, the two-row necklace. A lot of detail, it twinkles. The jet-black color is in-season, definitely, and you get the earrings once again, Mediterranean-inspired . . .*

Their voices were as soothing as drugs.

• • •

Her phone blinked with a text from Phoenix in the morning. *Have dinner with me tonight. Bring the haikus!*

Oh, shit fuck.

She didn't understand Phoenix. What *was* that last night?

Later, a number she didn't recognize flashed across the screen. She hesitated, then answered.

Jim.

There was a lot of static, and his voice sounded far away, but he said he'd be home the day after tomorrow. He said he'd lost his phone. He was always losing his phone, then calling from strange numbers.

"I'll make you dinner," she said. "Do you think you'll be hungry?" How stupid, she thought. How stupid to plan when they never, ever made plans. She cringed at her stupidity.

"I could eat, probably," he said, though he was hard to hear. Even with a clear connection, they weren't good on the phone. "I'm sure I could eat."

She shopped for clothes in a dying mall, then went to the grocery store and bought a lot of groceries. She was aware of being manic, but she didn't care, because she was so happy. She remembered the grocery store the afternoon before the ice storm and considered the dark place she was in—as if it were someone else that night, strolling aimlessly through the aisles with blank shelves.

She killed the TV. Blood rushed to her face when she found the empty box of condoms under the sofa. That night was a galaxy away, she thought, a galaxy.

She found her phone charger, too—the white cord knotted *behind* the bookcase.

She took a shower with the shampoo that made her hair smell like coconut. She wore tall suede boots and her grandmother's locket he liked around her neck.

She bit the whites off her nails waiting for the food to come out of the oven. She wanted everything to be perfect, all the way until they fell asleep tonight, their legs twisted into foreign letters under the quilt.

In the morning, they would read the newspaper in their underwear, the point being to find the strangest article. "This one," Jim said on the morning he left for Texas. "*Turkish Woman Awaits Trial for Beheading Her Rapist. 'I shot his sexual organ,' the woman said. 'He became quiet. I knew he was dead. I then cut off his head.' Witnesses described her walking into the village square, carrying the man's head by his hair, blood dripping on the ground.*"

Now her phone rang from another unknown number.

When she answered, static clouded the line before Jim's voice came on. They talked for a minute about nothing, then he said, "So, listen, I was all set to leave, then Agnes called"—who Agnes was, she had no idea—"with some new shows lined up, so I'm going to stay for, I don't know, another week or so. There's some shows . . . I met up with some buddies of mine from New Orleans and we're going to play together for a while." When she didn't say anything, he said he was late for practice. Then he said, "Don't be sad."

"I'm not."

They talked about nothing for another minute, while she waited for the line to go dead to let her heart bleed.

She took the food out of the oven and her arms felt like dead arms—like in a dream, when they don't work, or they work only in slow motion.

All night the apartment would smell like food, mocking her. She considered her options. She could pick up a shift at Viceroy, and make money. She could call Rachel or Chloe, but Chloe was already working, and Rachel had been so distant ever since she'd moved away. She didn't even have a cell phone anymore. They used a landline, and grew their own food like it was the 1800s. Okay, okay—not that far back, but still.

Ellie texted Phoenix.

"Do you really think he's coming back?" Phoenix asked. They were drinking weak vodka sodas and eating bread— which kept shrugging under the knife as Phoenix sawed away—on the restaurant balcony, beside the café. This was Ozark weather—ice storm one day, sixty degrees the next. They watched the earth thaw from their corner table. "I mean, really coming *back*, and living in Fayetteville?"

"I don't know," she sighed. She was tired of feeling crazy.

"I'm here for you," he said, touching her hand across the table.

Jim, Viceroy—none of it was sustainable. She needed to change her life, but how, and in what way? Maybe she could go back to school, like Phoenix. She thought of Rachel— how Rachel just made things happen. Abracadabra, now she lived in the mountains.

But Rachel would say no, a thing doesn't just happen, you have to force it to happen, and then by the time you get it—it seems natural.

Ellie looked over the iron railing at the people below. A pair of girls waited at the crosswalk. She watched a silver Vespa speed through a yellow light. On the sidewalk, a woman pushed a stroller with a shade while a team of runners surged downhill. When they broke, someone piercingly familiar appeared.

He looked like Jim. Jim's age—same height, bearded, wearing a gray T-shirt and navy blue trucker hat. She watched him stroll down the wet sidewalk toward the restaurant, toward her, his thoughts focused somewhere ahead on the street, near the intersection. He looked so much like Jim that, for a moment, she thought it was possible.

But as he neared the restaurant, she understood that she'd never seen this man before.

Still, under the weight of her stare, she thought he would look up. This wanting him to look up—it was a game at first, to see if he would, then it became a need.

Look. Look up, she thought, until she watched him disappear under the balcony, where she had to let him go.

THANK GOD FOR MISSISSIPPI

CHLOE

MARCH 2008

Chloe pushed her screen door open and stared at the futon in her yard. The initial brightness of the sun on metal made her eyes white out. She closed, then opened them again, squinting. Taped to it was a scrap of paper with TAKE ME in black marker.

Right. There had been a party at the fraternity house next door—the music still trembled against her walls when she came home from work at Viceroy around three—and they must have dumped a futon in her yard to impress each other. Like on Saint Patrick's Day, when they drenched the neighborhood cat in green-and-gold spray paint. The thing died cleaning her coat on the sidewalk the next day, swallowing all those VOCs.

Chloe sat down in the glider now and wanted to pull her hair out. It wasn't the futon, or anything else; it was just a thing she did. She pushed the long mass forward, a brown curtain around her face. She pulled the darkest strands, then the darker strands. She couldn't say why it was so pleasing to pull her hair out, it just was. She liked examining the roots between her fingers.

Her hair was thick and wire-sprung, so she could obscure the bald patches with barrettes and new parts.

Still, sometimes she felt like people stared at her head when she wasn't looking. In her next life, she'd be a blonde.

She hadn't meant to live next door to a fraternity house. When she'd signed the lease, it was quiet. Summer weighed peacefully down on the street. The apartment had been ready immediately—a plus. The landlord said the girl who lived there before had disappeared without telling anyone, the door wide open, the electricity dead. Now that girl's mail kept arriving, piling up months later—unpaid bills, fashion catalogues, a birthday card with sound. Chloe opened everything, why not? They were connected, she and this gone person.

Rachel and Rachel's boyfriend, Autry, wanted Chloe to come live with them in their house in the Ozarks. But Chloe was making decent money at Viceroy, and life in Fayetteville was okay, most of the time. Rachel told Chloe that the world was going to end if they didn't change their lifestyle, that science guaranteed it.

Chloe believed in science, and she did care about the planet. She composted and carried a purse made of discarded billboard material. She ate vegan, but she was also a regular American with a plastic water bottle and a car.

At the sound of footsteps, she looked up to see a frat guy twirling his keys down their shared driveway. He wore a pink polo with a stain down his chest and Ray-Bans around his neck on a neon cord.

"Hey," she called to him. "Is that futon, like, yours?"

The frat guy looked at the futon without mystery. Now she knew for sure it was theirs.

"Nah, I don't know," he said.

"Do you mind just taking it back, please?"

"It's not ours." The sun shone on his forehead, his tiny red acne bumps. "I'll ask my brothers, but it's not ours."

"Well . . ."

"I don't know what else to tell you."

After the dinner rush on Friday and Saturday nights, Viceroy turned into a pseudo-dance bar, open late, like the other bars on Main Street.

"Alcohol is where the money is," Lorraine told Chloe. Lorraine wanted to stay open late every night, not just on weekends. "You have to go with what's working. There's no need to reinvent—you know, to keep doing the wheel over and over."

They double-stocked the bar and cleared a dance floor, then strobed the lights. It was fun getting ready—like getting ready for a party—until the people showed up.

Chloe had just bleached the lettuce and put the non-rotten tomato slices back in the container when Lorraine pushed the kitchen door open so hard the salad refrigerator inched open. "Fuck Bruce," she said.

Lorraine could speak only in different shades of loud. When she talked, she looked elsewhere—at the wall some-times, or into the legs of an empty chair. Her personality was restaurant-acquired: friendly and two-faced and guarded, the way some people spoke to children.

Chloe understood how it happened. Sometimes after a busy night of being fake-friendly, she had to check herself, and remind herself to go back to her real personality.

"What happened?" Chloe said, not caring, but having to ask because Lorraine owned the place.

"Put it this way: Bruce is still waiting for Ellie to come back."

Ellie hadn't shown up for work in a week. Who cared? Bruce had a thing for her. So what? Who didn't? Honestly, Chloe thought, her whole life it had never been any different: A pretty face comes along and everything goes out the window.

Chloe hated Ellie. So *why*, she often wondered, was she always thinking about her?

Jim, the famous Jim, was playing at Natalie's tomorrow night, and Chloe doubted Ellie could stay away. They had broken up three months ago, but Ellie still rambled on about him every shift, then through her shift beers. As if Chloe wanted to hear. As if Chloe cared. What Chloe wanted to do was shove her across the room, pull her hair, kiss her, bite her—she didn't know—and say, *Look. He's a fucking musician! He has to travel. What did you expect to happen?*

For all the listening she did, Chloe had never met Jim. He had never once picked Ellie up from Viceroy, or drank beers at the bar so Ellie could forget to charge him. Bruce's joke was that Jim was Ellie's imaginary boyfriend. Like there was no Jim. Ellie did not like this joke.

Bruce and Lorraine lived on the verge of killing each other—or else they were in love, thinking about getting married again. Even when they were married, Lorraine told Chloe they could never hold things steady. "Hot and cold as a faucet, put it that way."

Before each dinner shift, Lorraine put in hoop earrings or pinned a flower behind her ear. Bruce changed in the basement from his lunch T-shirt into something worse—often shiny, with tear-away buttons. A thin gold chain shimmered around his neck.

Bruce walked into the kitchen now and Lorraine glared at him. He was wearing a bright tiger-print shirt that reflected color onto his neck.

"Ready for tonight?" Chloe asked him. She hadn't meant to sound sarcastic, she was only trying to slash the tension.

But Lorraine smiled at Chloe, before breaking into a laugh. "Nice shirt. I mean, really. It's *greeeaat*," she said, pointing like the tiger in the Frosted Flakes commercial.

"If you're mad about Ellie," he replied, "I'm only thinking of the schedule, whether to fill her shifts or not. Now, you're *welcome* to do the schedule . . . but I don't remember you ever once doing the schedule—"

She said she already knew everything he was going to say, then walked out of the kitchen. When she was gone, Bruce put his thumb and forefinger between his eyes and shook his head. This was for Chloe's benefit, she realized. He loved an audience as much as Lorraine did.

"Are you going to dance tonight?" he asked.

She shook her head. She didn't like to dance. A breeze floated from the back door and caught the metal fan.

"Why not? You could be sexy."

"No."

"Not as sexy as Ellie," he added. "That T-shirt makes you look poor."

"I am poor."

"Not after tonight, honey. What kind of T-shirt is that, anyway?" He touched the sleeve. "It feels like you're wearing the newspaper."

"I am. Sort of. It's like, recycled . . ."

"Sorry?"

"Recycled newspaper . . . handspun yarn."

He paused. "Whatever."

Guys wearing too much cologne flirted around the pool table with women in tall pleather boots and short denim skirts with rhinestones at the hem. Top-forty country whined from the speakers. The chords kept getting mixed up with Chloe's heartbeat. People coupled off and two-stepped around the dance floor.

All night she poured from the tap, ran trays of glasses back and forth. Started tabs, closed tabs. Somebody started a fight; Bruce shoved them out.

The bathroom was two stalls down a gone hallway with everyone waiting against the wall, the red tips of their cigarettes glowing in the cramped dark. When a girl passed out under the sink, everyone watched as Lorraine coaxed her, then dragged her to her boyfriend's truck in the parking lot.

It was a sad kind of crowd, but it could always be worse. The Arkansas motto was "Thank God for Mississippi."

After last call, Bruce poured two shots of tequila—one for Chloe, one for himself—because they'd worked hard, he said. But really it was an opportunity to exclude Lorraine. Their glasses hit and they sucked their limes.

"There's a futon in my yard," Chloe announced. The alcohol stroked her brain. "Somebody put it there. Like as a joke or something."

"So?" Bruce said. "Move it."

"It's heavy."

"Are you that delicate?"

Chloe spent the morning in the summer glider, rocking herself with one heel, with the circle of an empty day in front of her. She looked at the smashed mulberries around her feet, the purple stains. She should do something about all these mulberries. Take Rachel, for example. Rachel would make jam, or wine, or something useful like that.

The futon was still there with its TAKE ME sign—but TAKE ME had run off with last night's rain, so that only a few faded lines streamed downward like tears.

She put on shoes, then lifted with her knees. The black metal was hot in her grip, her fingers sweaty. She set it down and put her hair in her face. She started to pull the darker strands, one by one.

She brought the mail in. Two bills for the girl who didn't live here anymore, and a birthday card and book from Rachel. It touched her that Rachel had thought of her, since her birthday was still a week away.

The book was *No Impact Man.* Chloe turned it in her hand and read the back cover. A family in New York City swears off plastic and toxins, turns off the electricity, goes organic, and tries to save the planet from environmental catastrophe.

She felt a wave of terrible guilt—as if she were that fat friend, receiving a diet book.

She opened the card and read Rachel's words, hearing Rachel on the page, seeing her through her handwriting. A four-leaf clover was taped to a cloud of blue construction paper. Rachel had written, in floral cursive: *I found this for you on my favorite hill. Happy 23rd!* At the bottom she'd written, *Come Visit . . . We love you.*

Rachel had drawn a heart at the bottom, the kind of

heart she used to draw in the margins of her Western Civ. notes in college, next to her then-boyfriend's name over and over.

Rachel and *that* boyfriend used to repair bikes together at the High Roller Cyclery. They biked everywhere—it was their thing. Their bodies were hard little weapons of muscle. Once, they biked all the way to Chicago. And now? Now that didn't count. All that was all gone now—the boyfriend and the bike. Rachel was like that, always changing, always turning into something else.

Chloe swallowed a B12 for dinner, then arranged the barrettes in her hair with part of a joint in her mouth. No matter what she did, the bald spots showed tonight. She kept tilting her head in various angles toward the mirror.

She drew the wand of mascara over her eyes and dotted her wrists with lavender. She walked down the street past the El high-rise, past the patio bars with outdoor fans and the glass storefronts to Natalie's Majestic Lounge. All she could think about was that she wasn't green enough, she wasn't environmentally responsible.

Chloe paid the five-dollar cover, then held her wrist in space while someone snapped on a bracelet. She looked around. A hallway connected the bar part to the music part, where NATALIE'S glittered in old-fashioned bulbs behind a stage with various Persian rugs across it. A couple dozen people stood around, waiting for the music to start.

She felt like the only one who'd come alone. She walked to the front again and pretended to shop the merchandise. A stack of *8-Track Motel* CDs waited by the register. On the cover, the band held their instruments, legs dangling off a train car. She picked out Jim, the one with the banjo. Pretty much what she figured.

T-shirts cost ten dollars, bumper stickers five. A pair of red cowboy boots sat at the end of the table. They were men's, she finally decided, but still, they looked small and narrow. She examined the worn-out toe, the leather tongues, peace signs stitched to both heels.

The guy behind the table startled her by saying, "You like those?"

"What?" she said, putting them back.

"There's a story behind those. Phoenix Pace used to be in this band, and he wore these boots to like every show. He wore them everywhere. They're legendary."

"Oh." She looked at them again. "Okay."

"He went back to school, so he's retiring his boots." He pointed to Phoenix, who was standing with a group of guys wearing skinny ties and oversize glasses, drinking dollar cans of Olympia.

"I know Phoenix Pace," she said. "He comes into where I work." This was true; she knew him though Ellie. Ellie would pull her into the kitchen of Viceroy and say, "I know he's in my section, but please, please wait on him. He's really nice, I swear—I just can't."

"You can't?"

"Won't."

"Why?"

"Don't want to."

So Chloe would wait on him. All he wanted was a couple of PBRs or a screwdriver while he scribbled math equations on a legal pad. Sometimes he made up haikus on napkins, and told Chloe to give them to Ellie. "It's an inside joke," he'd insist, but Chloe could tell he was proud of them.

"So the deal is this," the guy was saying. "The new owner of the boots gets to meet Crush Heat Burn afterwards."

She almost laughed at the assumption that anyone who saw them—a local band, more or less—was dying to meet them.

But she did want the boots. "How much?"

"Fifteen."

"Dollars?" They were Durangos, after all.

"Well, they're used, and—it was Phoenix's feet."

She smiled.

"It's meant to be. He was hoping a girl would buy them."

This made her feel pretty for some reason, and lucky, and suddenly she felt glad to be out. She reached for her wallet.

"Want to wear them now? I'll keep your others back here."

She looked down at the blue-and-yellow laces of her New Balances and said yes.

She was feeling good now, different. The music was starting, and she enjoyed the *click-click-click* the boots beat across the floor. The lights from the stage iced the white fringe of her cutoffs.

Jim wore a trucker hat and rolled-up Levi's and a gray T-shirt with a cigarette burn over the heart pocket. He sang,

Down in the Delta, where there is shelter
No helter-skelter, no blues around

I'm on my way now, most any day now
I'm delta bound

Her pulse kept time with the song. The girls in the front row were calling his name, but his eyes stayed shut. His voice was deep and twangy. The sound was Texas swing, ragtime, country blues.

She became more aware of her pulse, which was now beating faintly, faintly between her legs.

She looked around for Ellie, her blond braid. She didn't see her. She orbited the crowd, looking for a pretty girl.

They played through most of *8-Track Motel*. They played a Lefty Frizzell and Mississippi Sheiks cover, then some new ones. They wanted to record another album soon. They played Hank Williams and Ralph Stanley. People danced to the murders of Pretty Polly and Frankie and Johnny. They played "I Think I'll Just Stay Here and Drink," and the song rushed to the tips of her fingers. But she didn't dance. She couldn't dance.

People kept buying the band shots of whiskey. The other guys were okay, but not look-twice appealing like Jim.

She never found Ellie. After the encore, she bought a copy of *8-Track Motel* with the ghost of his banjo still in her ears. Jim was signing CDs for the line. He was smoking a cigarette, the kind you roll yourself.

The girls in the front row passed him, pushing through the crowd. "Good show," one girl said, sliding by with her lips to her drink. A woman of Viceroy material walked by and said something he didn't hear, or pretended not to hear.

He glanced at Chloe, then signed her CD in one loose stroke. "You're the one who bought the boots?"

She nodded. "I'm Chloe."

He shook her hand. His hand was warm and calloused in hers. It was huge, but she could still feel all the bones. She thought there was something poignant in that, like a metaphor was there, but she couldn't concentrate. She would think about that later. She realized that she was still holding his hand.

She pulled away and shifted her eyes.

The fiddle player told him that everything was loaded in the van. "This is Dane," Jim told her, introducing them. "She got Phoenix's boots."

"Nice," Dane said. "You live around here?"

She nodded. "Around the corner." She couldn't think of anything else to say. Was *this* the meeting-the-band part? A girl with long black hair and a turquoise stone around her neck wanted her CD signed, so Chloe stepped out of the way.

"Thanks for coming," Jim told Chloe, over the pretty girl's head. "Be careful walking home."

But after she went to the bathroom and retrieved her shoes and walked outside, she saw him again. The whole band stood in a yellow cone of lamplight, looking around at the washed-out parking lot. The bass player was on his phone, arguing with a girl. Jim tossed Chloe a head nod, then looked surprised when she approached.

"Great show. Again. It was awesome," she heard herself saying. *It was awesome*—what a horrible way to speak. "What are you doing now?"

"Just waiting around, figuring out where to stay. The van sleeps two people." He nodded to the maroon van behind him. "And we have sleeping bags."

"We need to get some grease," the bass player said abruptly, shoving his phone into the pocket of his corduroys. "Where are the restaurants?"

"I work at a restaurant," Chloe said.

"Which one? Is it still open?"

"Viceroy."

She shouldn't have said anything. She knew better. She wanted to call it back because Jim was staring at her, as if seeing her clearly for the first time.

"My girlfriend used to work at Viceroy," he said.

"Girlfriend?"

"Do you know Ellie Williamson? She waited tables there—she—well, ex-girlfriend. I guess."

"Why do you need grease?" Chloe asked.

"The van," the bass player said. "It runs on grease. We play Eureka Springs tomorrow, then Saint Louis. What do you think?"

"We'll get it from Hugo's," Dane said, trading looks with Jim, as if in secret code.

"It doesn't matter where we get it," Jim replied. "We can get it here, there. It doesn't matter. Viceroy." He stared at the top of the maroon van like the wind had been kicked out of him. He turned to Chloe. "You mind if we crash with you? We'll go to Hugo's in the morning and get some grease."

• • •

They parked the van under her mulberry tree. The bass player took an Ambien and went to sleep in the backseat, but she and Jim and Phoenix's replacement and Dane sat outside her front door and passed the bowl and the lighter around. Moths flurried around the porch light. If she concentrated, she could hear their wingbeats. Then she stopped, because that reminded her of her mother.

She was eight or nine the first time her mother put her in the shower and pointed to the showerhead and said, "Listen. Listen. And tell me what you hear."

Chloe listened.

She didn't hear anything.

Her mother said, "No, really. Really listen this time."

How do you prove that you're listening? She remembered her mother's intent gaze as she listened again with an ear to the showerhead, desperately wanting to hear something, whatever it was her mother heard.

Then it was the electrical sockets. All the sockets in the walls were to be examined. Her mother unplugged everything and spent afternoons with her ears pressed to the sockets in the walls. "Listen, come over here and listen to this one."

"What is it?" Chloe asked.

Her mother brought a finger to her mouth—speak softer. "They're listening," her mother said.

"Who?"

"They're trying to kill us."

Then the voices in the showerhead began preventing her mother from showering, then going into the bathroom at all. When she had to go away, so did Chloe.

Chloe was sent to Memphis and lived with an aunt, now dead. At nineteen, she was on her own in Fayetteville, enrolled at the University of Arkansas.

Her mother had been beautiful. A blonde with a sharp jaw and heart-shaped face and gold rings on every finger. She was a tree of pretty scarves. If she closed her eyes, Chloe could smell the Chanel No. 5 on her wrists. What bothered her was that, in the old photographs she kept in frames on her nightstand, her mother resembled Ellie.

Frat guys were drinking on the roof, pitching empties onto the hoods of parked cars. Beer cans shimmered against the road. "Nice neighbors," Phoenix's replacement said. They lifted their instruments from their cases and played.

Chloe listened.

They yodeled. They played murder ballads. They played a Dolly Parton song, and she loved that Jim loved Dolly Parton. It was difficult to picture Ellie doing this—just sitting here, sort of disappearing into the grass, listening. The lack of attention would have killed her. She would have felt sickeningly ordinary. Maybe that was Ellie's one true thing, Chloe thought—that she couldn't stand to feel ordinary.

Jim played his new Wall Street protest song, "Worthless Waste," while fireflies blinked around the futon in the yard. They talked about the genius of the Carter Family, Sara and Maybelle Carter.

Phoenix's replacement said, "You're quiet, girl." Again they passed the lighter and bowl around.

"The quieter you become, the more you can hear," she offered. She didn't quite know where that had come from.

"What's that," Jim said. "Zen?"

"Hey, you're pretty," Dane said, very stoned.

Everyone laughed—Chloe the loudest; she choked a little on the smoke.

"No, but you are," Jim said.

She searched his face for hints of insincerity.

"It's understated," he went on. "Not everyone will see it. But the people you want to will see it."

"What's that," Dane mimicked. "Zen?"

Jim started to speak, then stopped. He tried again. "So— you know Ellie Williamson?"

She turned it over. She pretended to run the name through her head, as if, no, she didn't know Ellie. She wished she didn't. "A little bit," she finally said, staring at her boots, where the color faded at the toe.

"You work at Viceroy though?"

"Yeah, but I don't think she works there anymore."

"But—you don't *think* she does?" He stared at her. "I mean, where did she go?"

"I don't know, I don't think she's in town anymore." This was about as much as Chloe could stand.

He crossed his arms and looked into the trees. She changed the subject by complimenting the music again, how great the show was—just really awesome—how much she liked the boots.

"I'm going to bed," Jim said.

When the screen door slammed and he was out of earshot, Dane spoke up. "His girlfriend left him."

"Not left," Phoenix's replacement said. "She fucking disappeared."

"She was nuts though."

"Yeah. But still."

"*Still do-ing time*," Dane sang slowly, George Jones-style. "*In a honky-tonk prison . . .*"

"But seriously. She was absolutely fucking nuts."

Phoenix's replacement slept in the van, and Dane took the sofa. Jim was standing in her bedroom, where the floor slanted toward the wall.

"You might be uncomfortable," Chloe said, twisting the blinds shut.

"No worries. I have my sleeping bag."

He examined the map of the world on her wall. "I like this," he said, sliding his fingers across the ocean. He traced the reds and yellows of the continents, the black stars of cities. "I wonder where Ellie is."

Chloe shrugged.

"You know, for a second I wondered if she could be in the mountains, with Rachel and Autry. You know them? But then—"

"Yeah, they're my friends. They want me to come live with them, too."

"Yeah. They're generous. Were they trying to get Ellie out there?"

"I doubt it. Rachel loves Ellie, but Ellie would just fuck everyone there."

Jim looked at her in shock, then laughed a little. "Harsh."

"Sorry. That was mean." She smiled. "But I'm just saying."

He went back to staring at the map.

"I took this map from school one day," she said. "It was just sitting by a huge trash can in Driscoll. Isn't it amazing that someone would have just thrown it away?"

"Another man's trash . . . as the saying goes."

"Would you ever visit Autry and Rachel?"

"I talked to Autry the other day, actually. They've got a landline. It is gorgeous out that way, gorgeous country. Autry and Rachel make a good team."

Chloe laughed a little.

"What's funny?"

"Oh, nothing. I just think it's funny when people use the word *team* for love, or whatever. Like couples who say 'We make a great team' to describe their relationship. As if there were a score at the end of it all. It *is* cool they're living out there though," Chloe said. "Rachel knows what she wants."

He sat down on her bed.

The air felt very still. It felt weird to be talking this way to Jim, but also comfortable—like they'd been doing it all along.

He said, "Do you think Ellie knows what she wants? Or I guess, ever knew what she wanted?"

"I don't think Ellie knows what she wants—but somehow, I don't know, she has this paradoxical way of getting it anyway."

He sighed, then fell back onto the mattress. "You're cool," he said.

She thought he was kidding, making fun of her in some way. She turned and searched his face for signs of this, but didn't see any.

"I got the spins," he said.

"I mean—you can sleep here. It's no big deal." She touched the pillow he could use.

"Really? You're sure?"

She nodded.

He looked exhausted, spent. He looked in need, but of what, she couldn't tell. He stood up and said, "I need to smoke a cigarette."

She set out a tank top with thin white straps that crossed in the back, then stepped into the bathroom to brush her teeth. She resisted the urge to tug some of her hair quickly into the trash can.

When she returned, Jim was standing at the foot of her bed, staring at the tank top. He said, "Is this what I'm wearing?"

She laughed.

When he went to get a glass of water, she slid the tank top over her head, still smiling, and went into the bathroom again. She stood in front of the mirror to quiet her heart. She breathed for confidence.

When she came out, he was stretched out on his back, still wearing his clothes except for his trucker hat, which he'd placed on the nightstand next to her alarm clock. Its blue numbers—*3:33*—spread through his water glass.

She lay down beside him, trying to be very quiet and very

still. The box fan hummed in the window. White curtains blew around it.

He touched her back in the dark, where the straps of the tank top crossed. She lowered her head onto his shoulder, and inhaled the smoke on his shirt.

A train went by, and the water trembled in the glass.

She fought sleep, but it came anyway.

She woke once, with a sunrise already teasing the darkness from the room. She sat up and dragged the quilt over them. In his half sleep, his hand found her hipbone.

When he woke, he went into the bathroom. She heard the shower curtain slide across the bar, the hot water running in the walls.

Don't leave yet, she thought.

But with a few words, he was gone.

She was late to her lunch shift because she got caught up in a motorcycle rally. She pieced through the black-and-silver traffic. On the Harley beside her, the guy's T-shirt back said, IF YOU CAN READ THIS, THE BITCH FELL OFF. They wore bandanas and leather vests with big patches and wraparound sunglasses. Nobody wore a helmet, not one person, like a death pact.

Being late was normally okay—lunch was slow. But Ellie still hadn't shown up, and they still hadn't replaced her. So Chloe was busy as soon as she tied on her apron, when all she wanted to do was stand around and think about the night. She wanted to repeat the details in her head. She didn't want to forget a single gesture, or the bones in his hand, or the way he looked when he lay in her bed.

"Ellie, Ellie, Ellie," Bruce kept saying. "Ellie, missing work."

She wished he'd shut up about Ellie already.

Bruce asked her to call Ellie again. It rang until the voice-mail clicked on: *Hi, you've reached Ellie, I'm not here.*

She hated hearing her voice, even.

The deaf couple came in—Chloe's regulars. They wrote their order on a piece of folded paper, then slipped it to Chloe like a love note. She'd memorized their order months ago, but didn't know how to tell them this.

Lorraine knew everyone who came in for lunch. Bruce would stare out the kitchen's cutout window, watching Lorraine coast from booth to booth. She'd laugh with the regulars, refill mugs, make change.

"Listen," he said, to Chloe. "Who's Lorraine fucking? Do you know?"

Chloe was in the kitchen, waiting for the deaf couple's food. "Nobody. You? I don't know."

"Why are you so cheery today?" Bruce asked.

"What?"

"Why. Are. You. So. Cheery."

She shook her head. She fucking hated Viceroy.

She could quit. She could quit like *that.* She could go live with Rachel and Autry. Chloe imagined Rachel packing for her new life, happily throwing scarves and bathing suits and jean shorts into the jaws of her suitcase.

Chloe shook shakers of vodka for two pretty blondes, thinking of ways to contact Jim. She could join the Crush Heat Burn mailing list. But no, god no, that was stupid. It would be better to wait. Patience. He would be back again.

She gave the pretty blondes their vodkas and served the deaf couple their salads, which they ate in silence, rarely signing. They were just like every other married couple, Chloe thought, eating in silence. For dessert, they wanted spumoni. The problem when anyone wanted spumoni was that the ice cream was in the basement freezer. Not only was it where Bruce changed clothes, but also it was dark and mice walked in the walls.

She almost dropped the ice cream walking back up the stairs too quickly. She walked quickly like she walked quickly from basements as a child, afraid of the dead girls her mother said were in the crawl space.

She arrived home to the whole fraternity gathered in the shared driveway. They were all wearing navy blazers, casting a dark veil over the gravel. They listened to their leader shout his lungs away.

"From these honored Sig Eps," he shouted, "we take increased devotion to that cause for which they gave the last full measure of devotion—that we here highly resolve that Sigma Chi Epsilon shall not die in vain—that this fraternity, under God, shall have a new birth of brotherhood—and that fraternity of the people, by the people, for the people, shall not perish from the earth."

It was the Gettysburg Address! Kind of.

She looked at the mulberry tree, the tire marks on the grass. When she came home she walked around her apartment, trying to see traces of Jim—perhaps he left his trucker hat on the nightstand, a guitar pick on the porch?

Nothing. Nothing except his water glass beside the blue numbers of her alarm clock, her pillow that smelled of smoke now.

She sat on the edge of the mattress and watched the wind suck the blinds against the screen. She picked up his glass and turned it around and around in her hand. She drank from it.

She shook out the quilt to refold it, and something thudded to the floor. She went to her knees and reached for it.

Jim's phone.

She held it. She studied it. It was a blue Nokia—the kind that still flipped open. The casing was scratched. She tried to turn it on, but it was dead.

She slept with it. Before she went to sleep, and then again in the morning before she was totally awake, she held the phone between her legs and rubbed it back and forth until she felt the agony of gratification.

By the end of the week, Ellie still hadn't come back. *Stay away*, Chloe thought. *Stay away, please stay away.* She went around all day with Jim's phone in the pocket of her apron.

When Crush Heat Burn played Natalie's again, next month, she would give it to him. She would have to see him again.

Chloe and Lorraine were standing behind the bar when Lorraine said, "I have to let Ellie go. I have to hire someone else, I don't care what Bruce says. Do you blame me?"

Chloe shook her head. She didn't blame her. "Do you think something bad could have happened to her?" she asked hopefully.

"I'm not mad, but put it this way: She could have had the decency to give us her two weeks." Lorraine paused. "Bad? Bad like how?"

"Well, I'm just saying, isn't it possible that something really bad could have happened to Ellie?"

Lorraine shrugged. "I'm sure she's fine. She probably just decided to do something else. I've seen it happen over and over—you know, cycles of waitresses. Plus, I would have had to fire her soon, anyway."

"Really?"

"I think she was taking advantage of the company." She nodded her head to the kitchen. "*He* would never admit that. She liked to drink here. I think she was drunk a lot of the time, put it that way. Sometimes she hid it better than other times."

After lunch, Lorraine and Bruce stood in the kitchen yelling at each other like actors in a bad thriller. Lorraine told him he was a fraction of a man. Bruce called her a dysfunctional cunt.

Even the basement was better than listening, so Chloe rolled flatware at the card table by the foot of the stairs, where Bruce's shirts hung from the rafters like ghosts.

As she married the forks and knives, she thought about Jim. The night had stood up inside her for days, but she was worried that, with time, the whole thing could slowly disappear, as if it could begin to feel like it never happened.

Chloe thought about Ellie in her nowhereness. She thought about Rachel in her Rachelhouse in the mountains.

She remembered Ellie's last night at the restaurant. She seemed rushed and happy—almost manic. Laughing, she told Chloe she'd made out with the dishwasher in the walk-in freezer. She said this as they were scooping spumoni. Then, in a strange brush of energy, she stepped all the way inside the freezer and breathed deeply. A strand of blond hair still flew from one of the shelves of ice.

She was out of knives when something shiny like a token piece caught her eye under the step. Ellie's locket. She picked it up, and studied it in her palm. Once, after glaring openly at Ellie's chest for several moments, Lorraine complimented the locket. Ellie had then launched into her grandmother's tale— married at sixteen, dead at forty. One side was her grand-mother's young face, eyes already haunted, in grainy black and white. The other side was Jim's figure and banjo on a stage. The hook was warped; the locket had slid right off the chain.

Some teenage girls waltzed in late, their makeup smeared, sweating through the pinks and purples of their halter dresses. They were laughing, tipsy from somewhere else, wherever they disappeared from their dates.

Chloe stood by in a trance. She watched them through the hoop of Lorraine's earring. She touched Jim's phone in the pocket of her apron, and kept her hand there.

"Look at these prom queen zombies," Lorraine shouted through the music. "They're not twenty-one."

"Nope," Bruce said. "But they're funny. Let's give them five minutes of fun before we kick them out."

"Dance with me," Lorraine said, and Bruce took her hand. He flashed a smile that belonged to their secret language, and spun her into the dark glow of the dance floor. Like that, they were on-again.

Chloe poured someone another beer. She watched a man in construction boots twirl a woman with wings tattooed on her lower back. Around and around the cowboy hats went, the eye shadow and fake white teeth, shiny silver belt buckles gleaming off every other hip—everyone two-stepping counterclockwise, dancing themselves in circles trying to create a place they thought they belonged.

MR. LINDSEY'S ANGEL

ELLIE

MAY 2008

I t was lunchtime at the office, but Ellie stayed at her desk, taking apart an orange in methodical strips. Michael's other assistants were in the break room eating diet food from the microwave and discussing *Dancing with the Stars*. They didn't like her because Michael—Mr. Lindsey—did. They called her Mr. Lindsey's angel behind her back.

She and Michael were just friends. They'd said it so many times it was a joke now. Every time he left her apartment, they'd say, "We're friends, right?"

Michael's wife had picked him up for lunch, and when he strolled back into the air conditioning at five after one, he put a double-chocolate brownie wrapped in plastic on her desk.

She watched him walk down the carpet of spades and diamonds to his office. She watched him wake up his computer.

When she bit into the brownie, he asked to see her.

She stood in front of his desk with her mouth full. "What's the headcount for tomorrow?" he asked, leaning back in his swivel chair. Tomorrow was the annual office picnic at the Lindseys' house.

She put her finger to her mouth—one second—and finished chewing.

"Hurry up," he said. "I have an appointment coming."

She swallowed. "Fifty people, I think."

"You think?"

She nodded.

"You think, or *are* fifty people coming tomorrow?"

She smiled a little, because he was just messing around. He was humiliating her in a way, and she was letting him. This was just one of their games. It meant he was coming over after work. He walked around his desk saying, "You've got chocolate on your mouth."

He glanced into the empty hallway behind her, then touched her lip. "I need you to get my dry cleaning. I'll come by later and pick it up."

She looked at the clock. *1:14.*

"Don't get chocolate on my suits now," he said, and under the stares of her coworkers, she cleared her desk for the weekend.

This thing with Michael, it was just a joke. It was an enormous joke. Soon she would quit doing ridiculous stuff like this. When her real life started, she would quit humiliating herself with ridiculous behavior.

Alone in the elevator, she looked up over the doors at the light jumping the floor numbers. Then she was in the parking deck. Its walls of sheet metal shimmered under the motion lights like pocket change. Before she found her Honda in the dark gallery of cars, she went to use the restroom, which was always empty, the lock missing.

She avoided the restroom upstairs, where the other assistants pretended to confide in each other while looking at themselves in the mirrors. They would stop talking when Ellie entered.

But when she opened the door to the parking deck restroom now, a blonde in a black sundress surprised her. The woman was leaning over the sink with her finger down her throat. She turned around and yelled at Ellie—"Get out!"—before bowing her head into the sink again to vomit.

Sick, Ellie thought. She closed the door and hid behind a wall waiting for the woman to leave. She was sick of being confronted with this—what she and Rachel had started to call unhealth.

Michael's clothes waited on a hook on the back of her bedroom door. The ceiling fan was going, rustling their plastic sleeves, like pages turning. A tune had been running through her head, one of Jim's songs. His songs looped through her consciousness all day. She woke up with one song in her head, then came home from the office with another.

She opened her computer and Googled his image. Enough time had passed that it was safe to bring herself down. Only a couple of months ago, she was still avoiding the sadness, still afraid of what the sadness could make her do. Now there was enough distance to indulge it. She YouTubed videos of Crush Heat Burn. She knew it was stupid. She went to his website and studied the pictures, the videos, the tour dates—though she already knew them by heart. She knew they would be in Fayetteville tonight, playing at Natalie's.

Crush Heat Burn might, at that very moment, be hauling instruments through the hallway that connected the bar part to the music part. They might be opening their first beers, the aluminum tabs—*ping*—littering the cement floor.

Or they might still be in the maroon van doing the highway to Fayetteville, passing stabs of yellow and purple wildflowers in the medians.

She waited for Michael by streaming videos of Crush Heat Burn. She listened with an unbroken attention she never gave in person. She had been afraid for Jim to know that she thought he was talented. *Why?* Because he might find out that she adored him? And leave? He was gone anyway, so what did it matter?

Her apartment was furnished, but barely. Some of her things—rug and coffee table, breakfront credenza, wingback and vanity—sat in storage in Fayetteville. She had left a glass bowl overflowing with Meow Mix on the porch for her cat, and three pint glasses of water, because he preferred glasses to bowls, and hoped for the best.

Let's face it, loving a cat was too painful. Everyone knew cats didn't move well. This way, she abandoned the cat before the cat abandoned her.

Bentonville was only forty minutes away but felt farther. Much farther. Fayetteville was the cultural, university territory—KEEP FAYETTEVILLE FUNKY, the bumper stickers read—but Bentonville was something else. Bentonville was home to the Walmart empire.

Rachel had helped her move. It had turned out that she was driving to Fayetteville that weekend, anyway. "Getting a few things for the house," Rachel had said. She picked up Ellie in Autry's pickup, then drove them into the lot of Fayetteville Self-Storage. "Self storage," Rachel laughed. "Get it? Like you come here to store yourself."

"Like when you have to hide," Ellie said. "If it were only that easy."

"Sometimes it is that easy," Rachel said. "Look, Autry and I are doing it."

Ellie looked at her with interest.

"Why don't you store your stuff there, with us," Rachel said. "At least then you won't have to pay for it."

So Rachel took the dresser, a rug, the antique chest full of quilts, four Hitchcock chairs, and a green kitchen table.

Now she would have to visit sometime, if only to get her things. Especially the things she was beginning to miss—her quilts and her grandmother's jewelry box with earrings still on the inside hooks, a space for her missing locket.

When her phone vibrated, and *Bruce (Viceroy)* flashed on the screen, she silenced it. He was calling less, now that it was obvious she didn't work there anymore. He'd leave a voice message that she could delete without listening to. He called "just to say hey," to let her know she still had a paycheck there. Well, that's what happens when you leave without telling anyone.

At half-past five, Michael let himself in. He threw his keys on the floor where the table should be—one of his jokes. He wanted to find her a "real apartment" with "real furniture" but she liked her single room, with its kitchen no bigger than a kitchen on a train. A two-by-four was nailed over the sink with catches to hang pots. Above her, it often sounded as though someone were rolling furniture back and forth.

Venetian blinds threw lines of sunlight on the wall. They made fun of each other, until they kissed with something resembling passion. He told her to undress. He left his clothes in a pile on the floor, all except his belt, and told her what to do.

Afterward, they lay there making jokes in front of the three-channel TV. A special was playing on the Hillside Strangler. A female narrator with a British accent added the standard sophistication to the segment, while bodies were discovered on the hill and in the road, left in a Datsun. Ellie tried to imagine just coming across a body—seeing a leg, or a torso, or a hand in a ditch of weeds.

The pull string of the ceiling fan clicked in time with the song in her head. She started humming, but Michael didn't know the song. He had never heard of Crush Heat Burn.

She never mentioned Jim, or anything about her life in Fayetteville. When he asked, she invented things. How was it that it was so easy to be with some men? Why couldn't it have been *easy* like this with Jim?

She got up and went to the kitchen to mix the gin and tonics. When she returned with the glasses and the ice, he had her two stuffed dogs on his chest, their little eyes facing upward. "I know I say this every time," he said. "But I can't believe you're twenty-three and still sleeping with these things."

"They're not things," she said. "They're people. And they've been married for thirty-two years now."

"Oh, boy."

She handed him his drink, and they lay in bed with the pillows propped behind them. "This one's missing an eye," he said, rubbing his thumb over the empty socket. "Do you ever wash these things?"

"Why would I wash them?"

He gave her a strange look. She looked back at him.

"Oh," he said. "You're earnest. Because they're filthy, honey."

"But I just sleep with them."

"Oh, boy." He patted her head and laughed. "I love you."

He was joking about the love, but still, it unsettled her every time he said it. Their relationship was a massive joke. She was dead inside. She didn't feel anything. The minute things turned anything like remotely serious, she would have to end this.

"Tell me what's going to happen tomorrow, exactly," she asked. "I mean, at your house."

"You see, it's a party. What happens is, there's an agreed-upon time and place, like an invitation. The idea is—"

"Your wife will be there, and all. Don't make me go. Please. I don't act right at parties."

"Oh, come on. We're friends, aren't we? It will look suspicious if you *don't* come. She knows you're my assistant, my friend. I mean, we're friends, right?"

"Yes, we're definitely friends."

"To friendship then," Michael said, holding up his glass.

"To friendship."

They drank. Then he ruined it by kissing her softly on the lips. She turned her head.

"I know," he said. "I know, I know. But I love you, and sometimes I want to kiss you like I love you."

"Michael, you've *got* to stop saying things like that."

He brushed her hair from her face. She rolled her eyes. He caressed the nape of her neck and kept his hand there, and squeezed it hard. "I'll kiss you however I feel like it," he said.

This was more like it.

"What is Marianne like? I've never even seen a picture. You're supposed to have one on your desk, by the way. It's standard."

"You're going to tell me what's standard? That's funny. But all right, let's see, what is Marianne *like*." He sighed. "Well, she gives me a lot of freedom. Obviously, she doesn't know how *much* freedom." He laughed a little, then cleared his throat. "No, seriously, Marianne could be beautiful if she lost weight."

It occurred to her that Michael might be a bad person, and it had nothing to do with sleeping around.

He kissed her shoulder. "Tell me a haiku before I have to go."

"Okay." She closed her eyes, thinking about which one. "This is a funny one."

"A funny one. Let's hear it."

"The mountain cuckoo— / a fine voice, / and proud of it!"

"Oh, boy."

"This is another funny one. Well, I mean, *I* think it's hilarious. That wren— / looking here, looking there. / You lose something?"

He laughed into her shoulder.

From the open window of her bedroom, ankle dangling against the frame, she watched Michael disappear down her street in his black car. The relentless drill of the birds balanced on the electric wire made her nervous.

Streetlamps ticked on with the first stars and illuminated the parking lot across the street, where a basketball game was going on. The sound of the ball bouncing and banging off the rim, sliding through its thick metal chain, all made her nervous.

A tune was running through her head, dredging up a memory of Jim teaching her to two-step at a Wayne "The Train" Hancock show. She watched them dance in her head. Then she saw him onstage at Natalie's. She watched him from a dark and sticky booth. Girls tossed and twirled their blinking Hula-Hoops. These memories were like TVs flashing at each other, and the friction of the images made her eyes tired.

She fixed another drink, not bothering with the façade of the tonic this time. She never bothered anymore when she drank alone.

She stood in front of the mirror to examine what Michael had done. Looking over her shoulder, she inspected the raw, raised welts on her back. It hurt when she touched them; the pain was as intense as pleasure. Thumbprint bruises marked the sides of her neck. She was satisfied.

She walked around. She paced. She listened to a voicemail from Rachel. Ever since the self-storage weekend, Ellie was supposed to be considering a move to the Ozarks. "Just *consider* it," Rachel kept saying, until Ellie said she'd consider considering it. They hadn't spoken much since then. But they were like that—they'd drift nearer, then apart, then nearer again, never quite losing each other.

Ellie called her back, and Rachel answered on the first ring.

On Rachel and Autry's phone, there was a persistent buzzing in the foreground, like a third voice. Rachel told her about the genius of Autry, the amazing sex. "When I say amazing, I mean amazing this time. No joking around."

Because in college, whenever they developed crushes and slept around, they would exclaim that the sex was amazing. Then, after the crush was over and out of their lives, they would say, "It wasn't that good, honestly."

Ellie told her that she'd started an office job.

"An office job. An office job where?"

"In Bentonville."

She paused. "Don't tell me . . ."

"Yeah."

"Oh, no."

"I'm afraid it's true. It's for Walmart. What they're saying on TV is a fact. It's really, really hard to find a job."

"But Walmart? Ellie—my god. Walmart is an evil corporation."

"I know, but I had to get out of Fayetteville. I feel lucky to even *have* a job, Rachel." Ellie heard the judgment in Rachel's silence. "I just try not to think about it too much, okay?"

"What do you do?"

"It *sounds* kind of bad, but it's simple. We basically research developing countries and try to figure out the best places to put supercenters."

"Well, it sounds bad because it *is* bad. Bruce called me about a month ago, speaking of jobs. He wanted to know if I'd heard from you, if you were ever coming back to Viceroy. He sounded worried that something had happened to you. He said you just disappeared."

"I know, I should have told someone. I just couldn't face that job anymore. Not that it was even that bad."

"Jobs aren't bad when the boss is in love with you."

Ellie sighed. "Ah, well."

"Anyway, I told him I didn't really know, but that you were fine. Are you seeing anyone now?"

"No." The birds wouldn't stop. Ellie was not going to tell Rachel about this thing with Michael. The obviousness of it made it embarrassing. She'd been on the job two weeks when Michael came over to pick up his dry cleaning like some horrible, utterly clichéd joke from 1962. She couldn't believe she'd let it happen, much less *encouraged* it to happen. "Nobody," Ellie said.

"Autry said he's glad you broke up with Jim. He thinks

Jim's a good musician, but otherwise a douchebag-and-a-half. Have you heard from him?"

"No. He's playing at Natalie's tonight though. Crush Heat Burn is."

"I'm surprised he didn't call you. Surely he needs a place to stay. Ha."

"He's probably staying with some lovely idiot who tells him he's amazing and stands in the front row. He probably doesn't even have my number anymore. He was always losing his phone."

"You'll love again, you'll see."

"No, I won't. I'm very clear-headed about it."

"No . . ."

Rachel said that, as for herself, she was happy. She felt the most capable and strong she'd ever felt. She was fed up with life as a parasite dying in a block of concrete. Those days were over. She loved the country, the mountains. She and Autry were writing a book together. It was sort of an experiment, Rachel explained, a project, about living in health. What that meant, Ellie wasn't sure, but she was impressed with how well Rachel sounded.

In the morning, Ellie stood at the window in her underwear, drinking gin. Cars rushed back and forth. She bit her nails while the TV talked in the background. She put off getting dressed.

Eventually Michael texted her: *Where are you?*

She got dressed.

She drove past miles of flat green fields with horses standing inside the fences, then turned into the Lindseys' neighborhood—a constellation of brick-and-stone houses with paved driveways and brown mailboxes with last names printed on them.

She parked behind the other cars on the street, then stepped into the deadness of Beau Chalet. The houses stood as still and empty as dollhouses. Land surrounded the neighborhood in every direction, but lawns were sectioned off right beside each other into even green squares.

In the driveway sat Michael's black car, and another vehicle. Marianne's, Ellie decided—a gold SUV with a WALMART sticker and a FAYETTEVILLE TENNIS ASSOCIATION sticker.

The Lindseys' front porch was full of cane chairs, and heavy outdoor curtains pinned to one side. She imagined Michael here in the mornings drinking coffee, reading the paper, working out the day's secrets in his head.

She walked around back, toward the voices.

Michael was in the pool, laughing with another assistant in a peach scoop-back. She splashed him; he splashed her back. Women liked Michael. Ellie almost forgot this undeniable fact until they were in public, where his effect was obvious. They liked his good shirts and long skinny ties. They liked his smooth dark face, the way he listened.

As for herself, Ellie wanted big mangy beards, she wanted flannel shirts with cigarette holes. She wanted instruments and the smell of weed. She told Michael this often. So many people had impressed upon Michael that he was extraordinary that she felt she could say almost anything without hurting his feelings. Sometimes she made a game of this—how far could she go? Just how mean could she be?

He waved at her from the pool. She looked away and slid a mimosa off a silver tray floating around. She drank it, then picked up another one.

Outside the white curve of fencing, where the yard began, her coworkers stood around in khakis and sunglasses, sundresses cinched with wide belts.

Ellie looked down at her shift dress, the blue anklets of veins above her sandals—faint, but they reminded her she wasn't eighteen anymore. Or twenty, or twenty-two. She was twenty-three, and she'd done nothing. Would she still be nothing at twenty-four? Twenty-five? Thirty? Rachel was practically saving the environment, while Ellie was working for Walmart. This morning's gin twirled in her stomach.

"You made it," Michael whispered, dripping with the clean smell of chlorine.

She slipped her foot from her sandal and toed the water, cool like the water that trickled from the office water fountain.

"Let me introduce you to Marianne."

"Now?"

She wasn't tipsy enough for this.

"Oh, come on."

She touched her throat out of nervous habit, where her grandmother's locket used to press.

She followed him toward the blonde in the white one-piece, lounging in the chaise—and felt blindsided. *This* was his wife? His wife who needed to lose weight?

"Mare," he said. "Meet Ellie, my assistant."

Marianne opened her eyes and extended a graceful hand, a thin wrist of silver bracelets that sparkled with sun. This close, she was even more beautiful, and captivatingly old. She was thirty-five, Michael had told her. She seemed familiar, even. Ellie tried to place her and couldn't.

"You didn't wear a suit," he told Ellie, as if they were alone. "We could have raced and I could have beat you."

"Michael, please don't swim," Marianne interjected. "You won't be able to hear tomorrow. You know you won't. I'll have to shout for a week." She looked at Ellie and rolled her eyes. "He has a bad ear."

"What?" he said.

"You have a bad ear."

"I'm joking!" he boomed. "Jesus, that's the oldest joke in the book. Anyway, look—I don't have a bad anything." He smiled and looked at them for a reaction. Ellie stared back, bewildered.

Marianne said, "Great. So you *do* hear your phone ringing when I call you—those days you supposedly work late. You *do* hear me asking you to stop at the store on your way home." She winked at Ellie.

Ellie smiled uneasily. Michael stared at the cloud of water drying around him on the concrete. He said, "Good party, right?"

They both looked at Ellie.

Ellie realized she was supposed to speak. "Oh, yes. Great party."

"You need anything, Mare? You hungry yet?"

"I'm not hungry."

"You sure?"

"I hate spicy food. Everything you ordered is spicy."

"It's not that spicy."

"Yes. It is."

"No, it's not."

"Yes, it is."

A colleague called Michael away and introduced him to someone else, and Ellie looked at the roof sloping toward the pool. As another tray floated around, Ellie traded her empty champagne flute for a full one. She resisted drinking it straight down, but took a sip and complimented Marianne on the house.

"We've barely started working on it," Marianne replied. "I want to have this pool moved, back away from the house further. And we've got some awful carpet to get rid of in one of the upstairs bedrooms."

Then it hit her—this was the woman throwing up in the parking deck bathroom. Ellie remembered her blond head tilted toward the mirror, the look on her face when she turned around. Yes. It was her, for sure. If Marianne recognized Ellie, she gave nothing away.

"It's hard to believe we've been in this house two years already," Marianne went on. "Anyway, we'll be gone for the month of August. We go to Jackson Hole in August. My parents have a place there."

"Oh," Ellie said. She doubted he'd be gone in August. His work schedule was already full in August. Still, she felt a competitiveness rising through her frame, a jealous tapping on her chest bone that she didn't want to deal with. Because it didn't matter, she reminded herself. This was all just a joke—she wasn't going to be seeing Michael much longer.

But it was the same tapping she felt with Jim, at a bar, when girl after girl after girl would walk by giving him stupid looks, and she'd pretend not to notice, because she didn't want Jim to confuse her with them.

Marianne got up and toed the edge of the pool and it was impossible to ignore the bumpy track of her spine; she was that thin. She dove gracefully into the water, barely making a splash. When she surfaced, she swam to the side and heaved herself up the ladder. When Michael came over, he embraced her in a kind of hug. He touched her waist, caressed her stomach in a way that looked a shade unnatural. She squirmed away.

The food kept under little mesh tents. Ellie saw Michael fix Marianne a plateful of grilled shrimp and crab cakes with spicy aioli and zucchini bread. "Eat," he told her, setting the food in front of her. She waved it away, but he left it there anyway.

Ellie watched Michael as he mingled with his guests, playing host. She tried not to talk to him the whole time, but after her nth mimosa, time passing unaccountably now, she didn't care. When she saw Michael heading to the pool house, holding his glass of beer, she followed him.

She followed him into the bathroom and shut the door behind her. Their eyes locked in the mirror.

She said, "She's too good for you."

"Who?—Oh."

"I'm too good for you, too," she said. "But this isn't my real life."

"What's your real life?" He rubbed his eye over the sink, his face close to the mirror to examine it. His forehead almost touched the image of his forehead. He wore the open-mouthed expression of a woman plucking her eyebrows, and a wave of disgust passed over her that this was who she was choosing to sleep with these days, even if it was just a joke.

"What are you doing?"

"There's a gnat in my eye, or something." His breath clouded the mirror as he spoke.

"You're too old for me," she sighed.

"Oh? What if you're getting too old for me, ever thought of that? You're going to be twenty-four in a couple of weeks."

She laughed. Then she said seriously, almost to herself, "You're an idiot."

"Do you treat all your boyfriends this way?"

"Just my married boyfriends. Do you think that forty-one's not old? Because it is," she said, provoking him. "It's old."

He wiped his hand on his slim swim shorts and blinked at himself in the mirror. Then he crossed his arms and turned to her.

He stepped forward, as if to slip an arm around her waist, but instead he twisted the lock behind her. He kept his hand on the doorknob and kissed her, then bit her bottom lip so hard that she actually almost exclaimed. He bit her again to silence her. He pressed against her, and they kissed. "Get on your knees," he told her.

"What?"

She pretended to be shocked.

"Get on your knees."

She didn't move.

She rolled her eyes. "No means no," she said.

"Really? Then say no."

She looked at him, meaning, *here, please use my body, please make me not have to think.*

The sun was closing into a bank of clouds when Ellie thanked Marianne for hosting the party. "I should get going," Ellie told her. She looked at her wrist, checking the invisible time.

"You're leaving?" Marianne's face was red and puffy, and Ellie knew she'd just come from some other bathroom, where she'd been heaving her roots into the sink.

Ellie started to make an excuse about the time, that it was getting late, about deer crossing, but she trailed off. She didn't care enough. She needed to sit down. She tasted blood in her mouth.

"I'm sure we'll see you again before we leave for the lake," Marianne said. She leaned in as if to embrace, but then her mouth grazed Ellie's ear. She whispered, "You're an ugly little girl, aren't you?"

Instead of speeding away, Ellie drove slowly from their neighborhood, as if to punish herself. She denied herself loud music to blur everything away, the ability to escape. She passed her turnoff and kept going.

Now she sped up. She let the windows down. The stale car air was replaced with wind as she drove past miles and miles of fields and the wings of white fences.

The speedometer was quivering past eighty, eighty-five

now, ninety. Horses were flying over her windshield. The mansions and barns were flying over her windshield. She kept closing her eyes, to escape inside this short thrill. Then she would bring them back to the road, the speedometer, then close them again. She wished she could disappear like this.

She woke up with bands of pressure around her whole body. She was so tired of this—tired of waking up and thinking what the fuck is *wrong* with me?

She pushed the sheets away and went to the bathroom mirror. Her eyes were small and red and watery like two pieces of glass. Her knees and shins were purpled with bruises from the bathroom floor, and this made her feel better, the evidence of pain. She remembered sitting on her knees for Michael. She remembered driving very drunk with her eyes closed, topping ninety through the twisting fields. She could have killed someone.

She spent the day drinking at a chain restaurant. She sat at the bar, alone, looking at the ridiculous wall decorations. Outside, through the window, black-eyed Susans bloomed through the cracks in the parking lot. She wondered why people thought that life growing where it shouldn't was somehow hopeful. A tree growing in Brooklyn, for example, wasn't hopeful. Everything seemed disorganized and wrong, out of place and unoriginal. She drank steadily and stared at the people sitting at tables.

They had their giant iced teas and straws, and the normal day ahead of them, lined up with things like weeding and painting the shed. Whatever people did.

She daydreamed about earplugs that looked like hearing aids but blocked sound out instead of enhancing it, plus dark sunglasses that blinded her. She thought about various ways to live this way, by blocking out the life.

She tore napkins into bits, making a pile next to her Jameson. She looked at her phone. She started to pick the back of it apart, beginning at one edge, where the screen was already smashed—who knew how this had happened?—and took it down to its battery.

Bits of black casing were all over the bar now.

She examined the phone back. Written on the battery was the warning: POTENTIAL FOR FIRE OR BURNING. DO NOT DISASSEMBLE, PUNCTURE, CRUSH, HEAT OR BURN.

Her ringtone surprised her. Her disfigured phone was ringing—it seemed unbelievable that something this damaged still worked.

"Hey," Rachel said, when Ellie answered.

"Rachel?"

"Are you drunk?"

"No, I'm having lunch."

"So, look, we're looking at the calendar right now, and we really want you to come up for a week."

"Rachel, no, I need a lobotomy."

"What?"

"Do they still do those? I wouldn't sue anyone."

"What are you talking about?"

"I just want to quit thinking. I do. I really do."

"All right, well, coming here would be the closest thing to a lobotomy," Rachel said, as if she'd said this sentence a hundred times. "You can leave all your unhealth behind. You can escape from yourself here—I mean it. Seriously."

Her middle finger, where she held the phone, was burning. She had forgotten that the back of her phone was gone, and now she was pressing her finger on its chemical heat. A numbness spread down her hand, through her wrist. She switched hands and tried to remember.

"The natural world," Rachel was saying. "I'm talking trees and our huge yard, and there's a creek, and the river, and real stars in the sky over the mountains. Ellie, the clarity of the stars alone will make you leave Bentonville—that hive of unhealth, with all the diets and cancer in the lean cuisines and *Dancing with the Stars* and the Internet. You *are* what you see and hear and eat—don't you see? Why live that way, with no connection to your food, or nature, or to any of the things at all that make us alive and human?"

At the office on Monday, when Michael strolled past her desk, she could think only of Marianne. *You're an ugly little girl, aren't you?* She decided that she despised Marianne, and she judged Michael now for having poor taste.

"What's wrong with you?" he asked. She'd just stacked a sheaf of papers on his desk, and had started to walk away without saying anything. He'd been looking out the window, lost in the sun beating the car hoods on the street. "Close the door."

She paused, then closed the door and stood in front of his desk.

"Come here." He was sitting in his chair. She walked over

to him. He put both hands on her waist and pulled her onto his lap. "What's wrong?"

"Nothing." She looked at the ceiling, to make the tears in her eyes fall back into place.

"Tell me."

She put her head on his shoulder.

"Listen—" He touched her chin, making her look up. "Listen. What's wrong? I would blow up my life for you. You understand that, right? I would *be* with you."

She didn't respond.

"Say something."

"Why do you make Marianne think she's fat, and ugly and stuff?"

"Don't change the subject."

"Michael, I'm a terrible person."

"I don't know what that means."

The phone rang then, and he answered it. While he talked about money, one of Jim's songs played in her head. She started kissing Michael's neck, to silence the chords. He tasted like salt and she liked it. She licked it.

When he hung up, she reached for his belt.

He grabbed her wrists and brought them to his heart. "Don't change the subject."

She pulled away. "I'm about to start crying right now, don't you see? I'm an idiot . . ."

"Stop." He kissed her gently.

She didn't want him—couldn't he see that? "You don't know me," she said.

"I do know you. Why won't you let me in?"

Oh, for god's sake!

"What are you afraid of, Ellie?"

"I just want you to use me."

"No." He held her.

She fought this, hoping to be restrained, held harder, controlled. Instead, he let go.

"Stop. Stop for a second. Look at me."

This was the minute things became serious.

Her finger was still numb with the aftershock of her phone's battery. She couldn't touch it, although miraculously it still rang, charged, and lit up with texts. Still, she threw it away and this was a relief; it was like erasing part of her life.

All week, in a haze of alcoholic daymares, she contemplated leaving until she convinced herself.

She told Rachel she was coming, and no one else. She didn't tell Michael she wasn't coming to work on Monday, or ever again. She didn't know exactly how long she would stay with Rachel—two weeks at most. Enough time to put her bones back together.

She packed her things. She paid her last month's rent. She withdrew money from the bank.

It was warm and overcast when she left. There was something irresistible about leaving without telling anyone. It was like jumping on a train leaving town, tearing through the landscape, like the kind of character Crush Heat Burn sang about.

She drove through Harrison and Yellville. MCCAIN signs were staked in lawns, among plastic swing sets and bits of litter and statues of angels. A hardhat crew was at the end of the bridge that crossed the White River, and she fought the standard urge to drive sharply off the bridge. She fought the simultaneous urge to throw the car into park going sixty. Cotter, Mountain Home. She passed a little white church with PRAY UNCEASINGLY! on the marquee.

As she wound through the mountains, the sky cleared, and the purple ridge of the Ozarks sharpened against the sun.

She turned. Her ears popped. The contents of her life shifted back and forth in the trunk of her car. The farther she drove, the less like herself she felt—a wonderful, wonderful thing. Then the unmarked turnoff Rachel said to look for was upon her.

A long gravel driveway slanted toward their house. Dust sprayed the windshield as Ellie nosed the car into a space of deep shade beside two other cars that looked as though they hadn't been driven in a long time. A shed leaned heavily to one side, beside an affair of nailed-together wood scraps with a plastic roof.

She killed the engine and regarded the house: white siding with two glass doors off the back deck and a rose-colored tin roof. Rachel was standing in the huge yard, near a fence that wrapped all the way around it. Her red hair shimmered down her back.

Ellie smiled inwardly and got out of the car. The click of the door shutting sounded very loud in this air. Rachel waved from across the grass, and Ellie waved back. They kept waving like that, their arms making sense of the world between them.

IV

OUT BEYOND IDEAS

RACHEL

Rachel stood in the kitchen, shaking the starter for bread. Out the glass doors, the purple mountains bowed to a field and fence that kept nothing. But sometimes stray horses with flies around their eyes would come stand at the posts. A barking dog might tear through the yard with its heart in its tongue.

It was enough to remind them they weren't *completely* alone, because here were these animals, and these animals belonged somewhere.

On the ancient record player, a Flying Burrito Brothers song was spinning that went, *This old earthquake's going to leave me in the poorhouse, it seems like this whole town's insane.* She hummed while she palmed in the salt, the sugar, and the flour, then added sunflower seeds, for something different. She stirred the bowl on the green farm table—Ellie's green farm table from self-storage, stamped with cup rings and lined with the white stick of magazines. *Cause we've got our recruits, and our green mohair suits.*

The hardwood floor cried wherever she stepped, and this pleased her. It somehow corresponded to the image she'd been creating for herself.

It was a strange house, a sweet little house, jailed in floral wallpaper veined with cracks, and doors that didn't quite shut. A pencil could roll from one side of the house to the other. The bookshelf and stand-up mirror tilted as if on an ocean liner.

When his grandmother died, Autry's rich parents put off selling the house. ("They're *not* rich," Autry always corrected her, but they were—they absolutely *were!*) They hauled the "good" furniture back to Texas but left the few falling-apart pieces, and everything else, all the trinkets of two lives.

The deal was, Autry and Rachel could live here—for now—if they worked on the house, cleaned and took the furniture to Goodwill, or the dump, and prepared the house to sell. His parents had no idea *why* they wanted to live out here, but the roof needed fixing, the siding needed replacing, the boards on the deck were rotting. A plumber needed to be called, an electrician, a heating and air man, a Realtor. The area was growing; in a year or two, the acreage would be worth something, even if the house wasn't.

So far, they'd made no cross-offs on this list.

Nothing seemed too dire. Besides, they were doing their own thing. They had their Project. Autry worked outside in the garden, and Rachel kept house. They were just like one of those old-fashioned married couples you sometimes heard about.

Housework felt so feminine and throwback—so sexually retro. It was fun playing house. She liked kneeling by the mouth of the oven to watch bread rise. She liked pinning their underwear to the clothesline. She liked wearing his grandmother's apron with teal embroidery, and sitting on her knees to wipe wet blades of grass off the floor. She liked filling up old yogurt containers with the dead skin of food for the compost. She liked washing old Ziploc bags to reuse.

She'd been delighted to find this apron—what a gem!—still on a nail by the wall phone. The wall phone—yet another gem. Rachel realized that his grandmother had probably not felt so edgy and sexual doing housework, but the times, they were a-changing.

She heard footsteps, then felt Autry behind her, with his hands around her waist. He could hardly walk past her without fitting his hands around her waist, or patting her head. Rachel turned to face him, her hands like white magician's gloves from the dough.

Autry was six four and had to duck through all the door-frames. He kissed the top of her head, the part in her hair, and said, "Ellie awake yet?"—a joke, because when Ellie finally shuffled down the stairs in white shorts and moccasins, blond hair clenched in a braid, it was sometime after lunch. Sometimes she came down with the face of a bad night, but Rachel thought she was doing okay, mostly. Autry had her on a cleansing program to rid her body of her alcohol-induced poisons, her toxic demons.

Autry's beauty was continually confusing. Look at him once and he was this classic catch—tall, blond, and handsome—with blue eyes and freckles that darkened over his shoulders and the bridge of his nose in the sun. Look twice, and there was so much *more.*

This morning he wore khakis she'd scissored off above the knee for him, plus an Asian hat—the straw pointed kind. He pushed it onto his back after the sun went down. He wore suspenders and a T-shirt with a bearded man on the front, hang gliding. WHAT *WOULDN'T* JESUS DO? it read.

"You're wearing love blinders," Ellie laughed yesterday, as she and Rachel stared at him through the glass doors.

"You're just wearing cleansing blinders," Rachel said, putting an arm around her shoulder.

There was nothing to drink here, thank god. Ellie was edgy at times, especially in the afternoon, around three o'clock. Her hands trembled when she tried to be still, but she seemed content when she wasn't irritable.

"When are you going to tell her that Chloe's coming here?"

Autry asked now. He picked up a banana with a sticker that said ECUADOR, stripped it, then ate half with one bite.

Rachel sighed. "I'm waiting for the right time."

"I don't get it. I thought they were friends and everything."

"Ish. I think Chloe has some new boyfriend, anyway—so you'd think that would soften her edge."

"She needs to come here and get rid of the edge. She shouldn't submerge herself in unhealth."

"That's what I told her. And that we needed her, too." Sometimes it was tough living way out here in health, just the two of them. They needed other people for the Project. They needed company. They needed witnesses.

"Well, it's not that we *need* anyone," he said, between mouthfuls, suddenly exasperated. "I mean, we're fucking self-sufficient." He could be sudden like this. He swallowed. "It's just—this is an awesome place to live and people need to realize that."

"No, I agree," Rachel said quickly.

He kissed the top of her head, and she watched him walk through the glass doors. He folded the peel into the makeshift compost and rotated the barrel, then headed toward the bouquets of greens near the fence. They had cantaloupe and tomatoes—not producing yet—and yellow squash, and beans that twisted up two bamboo sticks tied together with twine, and green tubes of zucchini going thick, in the same spot where Autry's grandparents had them growing.

Autry had planted cucumbers and yellow tomatoes and herbs in two separate raised beds he'd nailed together. But only the cucumbers and Thai basil were coming up. Every time Rachel walked by, she picked a leaf of basil and ate it. She loved that.

They didn't know of any neighbors, except animals, and the chicken coop a few miles away. On a windy day, you could smell it. The closest house, a white cinderblock with boarded windows, was three miles down the road, a recently busted meth lab. A family of feral cats roamed the yard now; they cleaned themselves in the sunny driveway, listening for the movement of food.

She couldn't understand the appeal of all this meth. It was everywhere in these hills. She'd heard about meth from dramatic local news segments, but she didn't quite believe it. Now that she was here, she thought: Was there a drug that embodied less health, that made you look more like a seventy-five-year old anorexic?

At least when *she* took drugs, they were natural, not the chemical stuff that made your teeth rot.

She put the bread in the oven to rise and scrubbed her hands with cold water and baking soda. It was getting hot, but they chose not to use AC. Anyway, the system was out of order.

Vertical, office-style blinds copied sunlight onto their bedroom floor in long streaks. Seedlings grew in black pots everywhere, so the room smelled like earth. A glass bowl of notes she and Autry had written to each other sat on their dresser among packets of seeds and a tape measure and an all-natural deodorant called Crystal.

His grandmother had died in this bed. Sometimes, in the

blue-dawn of morning, Rachel saw the image of her corpse in Autry, sleeping quietly beside her on his back, hands over his chest, mouth open. He always slept this way, with his mouth slightly open like a dead person. What would she do if Autry died? This image, overlaid with the image of his dead grandmother, terrified her.

So she'd press against him, wrapping her bare legs around him. Then he would stir toward her with life, and the dead grandmother would, thank god, disappear.

She walked up the narrow staircase to the blue room, where Ellie slept. They called it the blue room because everything was—get ready—painted blue, as if for a newborn. The hardwood floors and the walls were blue, even the door was painted blue as a swimming pool. When she opened it, she found Ellie still in bed, writing in a black-marbled notebook with her two stuffed dogs beside her, hair spread on the pillow like a blond sea plant.

Ellie lifted the sheet and made room for her. Ellie's voice, her slightly sour breath, was comforting. When they were together, life was more comforting—life made more sense.

Across the tiny hallway was the third bedroom—pink and white with a shelf running along one wall. This was Chloe's room, but Ellie didn't know it yet.

They lay in bed together, laughing over ex-boyfriends. They liked to do their voices. Rachel listened as Ellie exaggerated Jim's country-Americana accent, softening the *r*'s, shaving the *ing*'s for drinking and hopping freight trains. "They taught me to yodel," Ellie drawled, "by going *little lady who*. Hey, Hank Williams got song ideas from cartoons."

Rachel talked abstractly about bikes, using tired metaphors about the open road. Her ex from the High Roller Cyclery used to talk like this. "Sure, Rach, we'll bike all the way to Chicago. If there's a way, we'll find it," she mimicked.

"They got their band name," Ellie said, "from the back of an iPhone. An iPhone, I repeat. And they try to act all old-school."

"The time I met him, everything Jim talked about was *gorgeous*. He overuses *gorgeous*. Like here's a *gorgeous* little tune. We drove through some *gorgeous* country to get here, man. Dude, the fiddle's a *gorgeous* instrument.

"With yours it was the phrase *right on*. Like, *right on, Rach!* Please. You know what? Jim claimed he had no idea who these girls were," Ellie continued, "these girls that came up to him after his shows—but he knew them. He *so* knew them. And he fucking encouraged them."

"I guess he does have to promote himself, sort of, in a way," Rachel said.

This was the wrong thing to say, she understood immediately from the way Ellie unglued herself from Rachel's arms, her eyes narrowing into tiny blue sparks.

Here was the difference between them with their ex-boyfriend talk. Ellie was still hurting; she was making fun of Jim to feel close to him. In this way, she was still holding on to him. Whereas Rachel honestly didn't care about bikes anymore.

She would never make fun of Autry.

She was crazy about Autry.

"Well," Rachel said. "Maybe one of his fans will get really hung up on him and murder him."

"This is how Selena was killed," Ellie agreed.

"It's how a lot of people are killed, when you think about it. People love stuff so much that they just have to go and ruin it."

Rachel looked at the amethyst on Ellie's nightstand. "Did you detox today, darling?"

Ellie followed her gaze and looked at the amethyst, too. "Oh," she replied. "Yeah."

"Ellie . . . Did you? Do you promise?"

Ellie laughed a little bit. "I said yeah."

There was a piece of paper next to the amethyst with Autry's handwriting on it.

1. Say the following out loud: I love waking up every day feeling the health and clear-headedness. Repeat until your intuition tells you to cease.

2. Rejoice in how happy, free, and natural you feel now that you are freed from the unhealth of alcohol.

3. Drink a full glass of water and imagine a beautiful, beautiful white light beaming outwards from it. Drink the water slowly. Feel the light pouring into your body with each sip, cleansing your unhealth.

4. Take the amethyst and cup it between your hands. Feel the white light circulate your body, becoming stronger with health, and then flowing into the amethyst. Imagine the crystal pulsating with the light of health. Sit with this meditation for a few minutes. Repeat until your intuition tells you to cease.

"You're positive?"

"For what, AIDS?"

"You're positive you're doing it? It's working?"

"I said I'm doing it, no? Come on, let's get out of bed."

Rachel twisted her body toward her. She felt Ellie's ribs in her hands as she held on to her. When she let go, she threw the sheet off their legs. "All right, yes. Let's pick berries. It's a beautiful day."

She hit tennis balls against the side of the house waiting for Ellie to wash her face with baking soda and step into cutoffs.

The wooden racquet was ancient—Billie Jean King–style—with a small head and tight beige strings. As a child, when her father and then-stepmother belonged to a club, she played ladder matches all summer, shaking up bright yellow Gatorade mix in empty Wilson cans between sets. In her next life, she might be a tennis star.

They beat a path toward the bushes at the edge of the lot, where three separate types of red berries grew wild. Ellie started picking from the first bush.

"No, not those," Rachel said. "Those are poisonous."

"These?" Ellie said, and picked a few more.

"Yes. Ellie, don't. See that hot magenta color on your fingers?" She sucked her fingers dramatically.

"Ellie! I'll have to tell Autry you're not smart, after all," Rachel said.

"Ha—he thinks I'm smart? That's funny."

They kept walking. They picked berries in silence from

the third bush, squinting. The day reminded Rachel of an expensive photograph, it had that kind of clarity.

"How did you even meet Autry?" Ellie asked, eventually. "I don't even know the story. How *does* one meet a respectable person?"

"We met at a black-tie party. Autry's like rich or something. Or his family is—I don't know, whatever. Isn't that kind of funny though? It was a fundraiser for the High Roller Cyclery—that's the only reason why I was there. I was working it. I was still with Dickface at the time, but I was looking for something else, something new. I met Autry. He was there with another girl, but we got rid of her."

"Once, I said *black-tie party* and do you know what Jim said? He said, 'Are there *that* many black Thais in Fayetteville?'"

"What? Oh, I get it. Musicians are stupid, Ellie. It's something you probably need to realize at this point."

"He's so literal. He thought *Things Fall Apart* was a breakup book. Like, a self-help, how-to-get-over-your-breakup book."

"Oh, no."

"Oh, yeah. Maybe I should read it," Ellie laughed. "Autry's great. I love him. I mean—you know, not like that. You know."

"That makes me happy." It did. As far as the *not like that* part—Rachel knew that. In her own strange, sometimes twisted way, Ellie was actually loyal. Cheating didn't mean having sex, anyway. It meant . . . she wasn't sure what it meant, but it had something to do with your soul, not sex.

• • •

The next morning, Rachel lay with one leg twisted over her body in the floor of the great room, trying to crack her back. Thick bars of dust floated in the room's sunlight. She was sore from planting colorful flags in the dirt all morning, marking the natural contours of the yard. While Ellie slept in, she and Autry moved debris and dirt around to train natural slopes for an efficient drainage system.

They called it the great room because it was really great. Also, big. Red clay pots baked on the sills of tall windows where the language of clouds went by, the sunsets, the blue moons. They imagined the great room as an ongoing argument between his grandmother and grandfather—he wanted an addition, she didn't. And after he died, she felt guilty, and went all out. The addition was larger than the actual house, which otherwise had low ceilings and dark wood paneling.

All her life Autry's grandmother was a conservationist; she was elected to the county board in the seventies when it was unheard of for a liberal to win in these hills. But at the end of her life, she went moderate. Her son, Autry's dad, ended up working for an oil company in Texas. Maybe she thought: Why bother?

Autry wanted to talk about the environmental influence and heroism of his grandmother in the book he was writing.

The phone rang. Rachel walked into the kitchen, knowing it was Chloe calling. She stared at it, letting it ring its ancient alarm.

She liked Chloe, she did. She loved Chloe. She did! But let's face it, you couldn't joke around with Chloe. It just wasn't *fun* like it was fun with Ellie.

She felt guilty the moment the phone stopped ringing. She dialed Chloe back. She stood there with the phone pressed to her cheek, and gave her directions to the house.

Rachel loved the landline—there was something so throwback about flinging combinations from one house to another, while she slinked around the kitchen in her apron.

When she hung up, she lay on the floor, warm with sun. She closed her eyes. She felt as though she were lying on heated bulbs, which made her think of tanning beds. Tanning beds—imagine! The unhealth was grotesque. Back in college, she and Ellie used to tan at Native Sun.

"Native Sun," they'd say. "Where Richard Wright tans." This used to kill them; they'd laugh.

They'd close the lids to their beds shaped like coffins, wearing their little black plastic eyewear. They'd feel for the radio switch on the wall, then fall asleep burning.

It was almost impossible to comprehend now, how she could have done such a thing. How could that Rachel, lying in a tanning bed, be this Rachel, lying on the floor? It made no sense.

Once Chloe had told her that every seven years the body is made of entirely new material. It made Rachel look into her hands, the network of pink lines in her palms, the blue veins in her wrists, and wonder *Who am I really?*

All that mattered, she told herself, was who she was right now.

Autry walked into the room and stood over her. "Ellie still asleep?"

"Ha ha."

He got to his knees and lay down beside her with his head on her chest. This made her back hurt, but she liked his temple against her heart.

"How's your back?" he asked.

"Actually—"

"Why is Ellie still fucked up over Jim? He's a good musician, but the guy's a dick."

"Tell *her* that."

"It won't mean anything until she figures it out for herself."

Autry had cooled on Jim because Jim kept putting him off about a visit. Sometimes he'd seem very interested in coming, as though he were nearly on his way, but he wouldn't say yes and he wouldn't say no. He wouldn't commit, finally—and Autry was tired of people who weren't all-or-nothing like himself.

"You were right, by the way," Rachel said. "You know how you told me to tell her that you thought she was smart? I told her, when we were outside yesterday picking berries. I always thought she knew she was smart."

"Beautiful women always think they must be stupid. You're an anomaly. You have beauty *and* brains *and* personality *and* you don't need anyone to tell you."

She blushed.

He could still do this to her: make her blush. She looked at her nails so he wouldn't see. She liked that her nails were dirty, anyway; there was earth under them.

He lowered his head onto her stomach, which made her back hurt not more, but differently.

"You're the only girl for me," he said.

She stroked his hair. He stroked her cutoff shorts with the pockets coming through. He kissed one of the pockets, while she stared at the ceiling.

"This room reminds me of the seventies," she said. She pictured a Roll-A-Rama roller-skating party with Sonny and Cher. She pictured green shag carpet, and swingers with mustaches. Its openness, the shape of the room, all called up the seventies, but, in fact, it was built in 1989. "It's funny that it was built in the eighties instead of the seventies."

"It's not that unusual," Autry replied. "If you think about it. The sixties didn't come to Arkansas until the seventies, and so on and so on."

He looked into her eyes while he undid the button and zipper. He lifted her hips to slide down her shorts and she winced pleasurably. She opened her legs and felt his soft tongue like a chord charging through her body, and she died a little.

"I don't mind at all," Ellie said. She sat up in bed. "The more the merrier. Where do you get that Chloe and I aren't friends anymore?"

"I don't know—It's just in the air, I don't know," Rachel said.

"Well, you're wrong."

"Okay. I'm sorry, I'm wrong."

They were lounging in Ellie's bed with the window wide open. "What are you writing in the notebook?" Rachel asked.

"I really don't understand why you'd think I would mind that Chloe's coming."

"Okay, darling. I get it."

The breeze slammed the door shut. "I'm writing haikus—or haiku. I'm not really sure how you say it plural."

"Can I read them?"

"No . . . well, not yet. They're all about being here though, in nature. And—health. I mean, to be totally honest, I can't believe how drunk I used to be. And hungover. Constantly one or the other. An awful cycle of escape, despair, escape, despair. Add a little self-hatred and utter panic into the mix. Anxiety that you feel in your head and physically, in your chest, like you're being crushed."

"The detox is working!"

"Sure. Ray, are there any other secret arrivals you want to tell me about?"

"Autry's invited a few friends, just some guys he used to play music with, and hike with and stuff. Nothing definite yet."

"He didn't invite Jim here, did he?"

"No," she lied. "Not Jim."

They heard Autry downstairs in the kitchen, clanging around. Rachel wondered what he needed. "Come on," she said. "Let's cook breakfast. Autry's hungry, I want to fix him something."

"Girlfriend of the year." Ellie stretched her arms. "I've never been down this early."

"You should try it more often."

"Tomorrow I could make breakfast, I guess. Because that's how much I love my best friend Rachel Kline."

"Ray."

"Who goes by Ray now."

Rachel sat at the edge of the messy bed and watched Ellie pick a shirt off the floor—red-and-blue plaid, with collar stays and two pockets over the chest. She held it up; it was Autry's.

Their clothes were mixed up, and everywhere. Rachel didn't fuck with clothes—she ignored that part of housework. Ellie slipped it over her head, and the shirt fell to the top of her thighs. She started to button the first button, then stopped. "Something's different," she said. "It's backwards. The buttons are on the wrong side."

"Men's shirts always have the buttons on the opposite side," Rachel said. "Do you know *why* men's shirts always have the buttons on the wrong side?"

"Why?"

"Because when the shirt people started making shirts, they assumed that someone else would be dressing the woman—like a servant—so they made it opposite."

"Oh. Lofty."

Ellie walked to the edge of the bed, and stood in front of her. Rachel played the servant and buttoned Ellie's shirt slowly for her. "There," she said.

"Thank you, Rachel."

"For what?"

"I don't know, nothing, all of it. I really don't know. Thank you for letting me escape here."

The deck circled the house, then spread into a platform outside the glass doors. The boards were warm and soft—they were rotting—under Rachel's bare feet.

She mixed yesterday's berries into the muffins. She brewed

coffee, then made it precious by serving it on a tray with white shards of rock from the river as stirrers. She served Autry first, then Ellie, then herself.

They sat in the outdoor furniture—Ellie's outdoor furniture—a black wrought-iron table that looked into the face of the purple mountains, with four chairs around it that bounced.

The day was already warm—almost hot. This afternoon it *would* be hot. Soon it would be hot every day. The season of walking around in cutoffs and bathing suits, and swimming in the White River and sleeping under stars, was practically here.

They talked over breakfast.

Then Autry handed Ellie a note, scrawled in his familiar handwriting, on a piece of torn loose-leaf. Rachel, pleased, read over Ellie's shoulder:

> *E,*
>
> *Out beyond ideas*
> *of wrongdoing and rightdoing*
> *there is a field.*
> *I'll meet you there.*
> *A*

Ellie looked up and smiled. "Rumi?"

He squinted, uncomfortable. "No, I wrote it. Let's take a walk," he said.

She scratched a bugbite on her inner wrist. "Do I need shoes?"

"Does she need shoes, Ray?"

"Yes, she needs shoes." She knew they were going to follow the path off the property, under a row of trees, then to a field.

There would be more stray horses with flies around their eyes like stars. Keep going, and the field opened to a spectacular view of the mountains. "There're shoes in the great room."

Rachel would wait for Chloe, and greet her alone. This was the plan. She would drop a little white-hot bomb of love on her without the distraction of Ellie. *Probably let Chloe get used to things on her own*, Autry told Rachel that morning.

She waited on the back deck, eating a chilled cucumber, bouncing in her chair to the rhythm of her thinking. A paper wasp traced the air before steadying over the bushes. Rachel watched it with intense concentration, though she was thinking about the moment before you come, how amazing it is.

She was having so much fun, she hoped Chloe wouldn't ruin it. But they did want Chloe here, they did—they did! Once Chloe was here, they could really devote themselves to the Project. They needed at least four people to start a movement, Autry said.

When she heard an engine in the distance, she stilled herself to listen. She heard it slow on the gravel. First she saw dust, then the Camry, then Chloe's face behind the wheel, through the streaked windshield.

Rachel watched Chloe nose in front of the shed, in the space between Autry's out-of-gas pickup and Ellie's dead Honda. The timing belt broke at 178,000 miles. Ellie didn't know that timing belts needed replacing.

Ellie was upset, at first, then oddly elated. Not having a car anymore was another form of erasure, she said, like throwing away her phone, like deactivating her email address. It was one less choice she had to make: coming or going.

The gravel dug into Rachel's bare feet as she hobbled to the car to meet Chloe.

Chloe pulled herself out of the car, pushing her sunglasses into her hair. She looked around and smiled, then they hugged.

Rachel was alarmed at Chloe's appearance. She seemed to have taken on the appearance of an eleven-year-old boy. Her hipbones jutted out like fins. She wore a cream-colored T-shirt with a bird on the chest, her pale arms coming out of it as thin as dolls' arms. Something very strange was going on with her hair. Was she going bald?

"You look great," Rachel said. "Really great. Stunning."

"Oh. Really?"

They hugged again. She felt Chloe's shoulder blades through her shirt.

"Thanks."

"How was your drive?"

"I never would have found it without your directions, if that's what you mean."

"Yeah, isn't it great? So far away from the madness."

Chloe looked around and smiled. "It's beautiful."

"Let me get these," Rachel said, reaching for the three vintage Samsonite suitcases in the backseat. She led her through the glass doors, into the kitchen, through the great room, then upstairs into her pink bedroom. She set the suitcases down in the corner and complimented Chloe's purse.

"It's made of discarded billboard material," Chloe said.

Rachel tossed it a second look and then discovered she actually did like it.

There was something Rachel had to ask, and she wanted to get it over with. "Listen—is it okay, Chloe, if Autry borrows your car later, to go into town and get a few things?"

"Oh, sure," she said, taking her keys out of her purse and handing them over.

She took her phone out of her purse, too, and looked at it as she spoke. "I brought a ton of food and stuff. Everything you asked me to get. It's all in the trunk." She looked helplessly at Rachel. "Is there no cell phone service here?"

"No, didn't I tell you that?"

"No."

"Well, there's a phone downstairs. We like it this way. Why? Who do you need to call?"

She looked up worriedly. "I mean, I didn't know I wouldn't be able to get texts or anything."

"Who do you need to call, your mystery boyfriend?"

Chloe blushed.

"The landline's downstairs, Chloe. Use it anytime you like—the bill goes to Autry's folks. Who do you need to call?"

"Autry's folks?"

"Yeah. They sort of own the house."

"Oh," she said, disappointed. She must have thought *they* owned it; Autry liked to give that impression.

"I'll let you get settled, and take everything in. Let me know if you need anything, anything at all."

Chloe gave her a fragile smile from the edge of the bed, holding her phone.

• • •

Dinner was almost ready when Chloe reappeared in the kitchen. Rachel mixed a salad and shook dressing in an old jam jar, then served pasta colored with squash and a pesto from the basil she'd spent the afternoon laboring over, handing the spoon to Autry and Ellie for tastes each time they cruised by.

"Are you guys vegetarians now, then?" Chloe asked.

"By circumstance," Ellie said, with a laugh. "Are you still vegan?"

"I *was* . . ."

"Not anymore," Autry winked. "Unless you want to starve."

She looked worried for a moment.

"I'm just kidding."

They all made a big deal over her arrival, all through dinner. "*Mi casa, su casa*," Autry kept saying.

"We're so, so glad you're here," Rachel said.

After dinner, they played records and smoked weed. They sat on the floor, and Autry began to speak about the Project.

"The manuscript will chronicle our way of life in health here," he said. "I think it could really change lives—I think we're onto something. I think we could start a movement." He wanted to write about how these four people—he looked each of them in the eyes—found peace and health in the chaos of a cruel, disconnected world, and found inner and environmental health by living simply and rurally. He wanted to call it *One Year, Four People: How to Find Health*. They would write the book first, of course, but he was already thinking big—maybe a movie, a tour, who knew?

"A whole *year*?" Chloe asked.

"I never want to leave," Ellie replied.

"You've got to trust me," Autry said. "Do you trust me?"

"Never," Ellie repeated.

Autry stared. "You don't trust me?"

"I never want to leave," Ellie said, raising her arms in innocence. "That's what I meant."

"All right. So it's the four of us from now on," he went on. "You won't even have to think about it—just let yourself go. Be true to your health. I've got you."

Chloe looked at Rachel; Rachel looked back and nodded emphatically.

"There're four basic tenets of the Project. Tenet One: The grandmother of all rules, so to speak, in honor of my grandma, is to make as little trash as possible. Like, not buying anything with packaging. Not making any waste that isn't compostable," Autry said. "Tenet Two, we'll grow as much of our own food as possible. Tenet Three, we reduce our household energy consumption as much as possible. And finally, ya'll, Tenet Four, we actively participate in trance meditation to find our inner, personal health."

Rachel nodded, in love with the Project. She thought about earlier, on the floor, the way her legs shook around his shoulders. There was a similar pulse beating inside her right now, listening to him. She couldn't stop looking at his tongue.

The record finished and stilled into place. "We're really starting something good here," Autry said earnestly. "It's a way of life—if we can get others onto it, too—I mean, we could legit like, save the planet, I'm just saying."

Moments later the sound of static came from the record player. Ellie, Rachel, and Chloe each looked over at the record player. They stared at the invisible static as if it were full of secrets.

"Hello?" Rachel said.

Ellie burst into laughter. They were high, definitely.

Ellie didn't smoke that often, and Rachel loved when she did. Her laugh was contagious.

"Actually," Ellie said, composing herself. "Thomas Edison thought the phonograph would help us talk to dead people."

Rachel looked at her in all seriousness, then started laughing.

"I'm serious," Ellie laughed.

Chloe wasn't laughing. She even seemed moved at the idea that the phonograph would help a person reach the dead. She stood up and walked to the record player.

"I heard you were writing haiku, Ellie," Autry said, rubbing the beginnings of his ironic mustache.

Ellie glared at Rachel, then looked away shyly. "I mean—they're haikus. But they're not good, or anything."

"The plural," Autry said, "is actually *haiku*."

"Oh. Well. They're literally laughable compared to the Eastern masters of the form."

"Aren't some of those haiku funny though, therefore making them literally laughable?"

She smiled reluctantly. Rachel swallowed her awesome laughter.

"I was just thinking," he went on. "Ray said they were about here. I mean, if they're good, and they're about finding health here, then why not include them in the book?"

"I don't know—they're more just for me—I—" She laughed nervously. "I mean, if you really want to read them . . ."

"Of course I want to read them, they're written by *you*."

She started to say something, then quit. She stood up and paced to the window in pleased agitation. She announced that she would do the dishes. But she kept her spot by the window. They spent the rest of the night reading passages aloud from *Give It Up!: My Year of Learning to Live Better with Less* and *What Would the Buddha Recycle?: The Zen of Green Living.*

By the end of it, Rachel was in Autry's lap, turning the pages for him.

Ellie was asleep on the floor, her head propped on a pile of bleach-stained towels, arms by her side, legs locked at the ankle.

Chloe was nestled beside Autry, her head on his shoulder, reading the words as he read them aloud.

When Chloe *finally* said good night, telling them how happy she was to be a part of something, and went upstairs, Autry put his hand between Rachel's legs, her jean shorts damp with sweat and heat.

He played with strands of her hair, pushing them behind her ear, while she kissed him. She put her hand on his thigh, over the fringe of his cutoffs. It was all ahead of her, she thought, as they moved onto the floor. In his eyes, she saw her eyes, and she felt the fierce and tender animal-beating of his heart against her chest.

When they had their clothes off, Ellie's leg moved. Rachel watched it with one eye. It was the *way* it moved that she knew she was awake. And Ellie knew she knew she was awake.

Neither of them cared. It was an experience. "Yeah," Rachel whispered, to everyone in the world, and nobody in particular. "Yeah, yeah, yeah," she repeated, and repeated again, until the words lost their meaning and she was deep within the house of her own body.

V

THE QUIETER YOU BECOME

CHLOE

AUGUST 2008

Chloe sat in a chair on the back deck wearing a cotton sheet around her neck. Sun stained the deck in gold all around her as Rachel and Ellie stood behind her head, trading turns with the straight razor. They posed their critiques in soft monosyllables, dragging the whole process out. *They* were having fun.

There was the click of the razor, now and then, against the glass bowl of water, cloudy with lathered beeswax soap. When Chloe concentrated, the little clicks sounded like someone knocking on the door of her skull. She kept hearing it this way.

The breeze swept strands of hair off the deck. She missed it already, her hair. She missed the barrettes and tortoiseshell comb she used to part it.

But she—she who had compulsively pulled her hair out, and not just the darker strands anymore, but tearing it at the root—had no right to feel sad *now*, Autry told her.

What had caused such angst and tension now had a resolution—they would just shave it all off. Rachel suggested it last night, inhaling weed through an apple, that they would shave her head.

"There's this thing I like to say, that I came up with," Autry added, taking the apple. "Tension is who you think you should be, relaxation is who you are."

Chloe slapped a mosquito off the back of her left hand. Her touch lingered there like a ghost. She closed her eyes and found herself among the network of sun-stars at the back of her eyelids. "We really should have donated all this hair to Locks of Love," Rachel said. "We're wasting it."

"I think they like it cut off in a ponytail," Chloe said. She'd considered it before. "And then they need at least ten inches."

"Let's be honest, Abe," Rachel said. "Who would want this hair? It's full of unhealth. No offense."

Chloe tried not to think about the mosquitoes, though her

skin was mapped in bites. Her forearms itched with poison ivy that wouldn't go away.

"Did you know," Rachel said, tapping the razor against the glass bowl, "that a head of human hair can support the weight of two elephants?"

"Well," Ellie said, "not this hair," and Rachel laughed.

When they were finally finished, Chloe raised her arm to touch her head.

"No, wait," Ellie said, and Chloe swore—swore—she could *hear* the glance they exchanged behind her. She was getting this ability. "I just mean, simply—that it might freak you out to touch it—you know, before you see it."

Chloe shrugged off the sheet, thinking that she couldn't possibly look worse that she did before.

Ellie and Rachel followed her through the glass doors; their steps woke up Autry on the kitchen floor—the coolest place in the house to read. Resting on his chest was a book with a red barn on the cover called *Back to Basics: The Complete Guide to Traditional Skills*. Chloe had read that one. Well, she had started it.

She was supposed to be reading a book now about starting and transplanting seedlings, but instead she'd stolen a book from his grandmother's shelf of novels called *The Member of the Wedding*.

Chloe confronted the bathroom mirror and took a deep breath. She touched her head, which felt as smooth and innocent as something just-born. Like someone else's head. Touching it, she felt like someone else.

The only surprise was the slight shine. It reminded her of the shine on the hospital floor where her mother had lived and died. Now her mother's slim figure walked in her head, down the shine of the hospital floor, while a nurse padded by on shoes like white erasers. Her mother led Chloe to the bathroom, to the showerhead, saying, *Listen.*

There's nothing there, Chloe thought. There was nothing there, she kept thinking, and her mother wilted back into background. She blinked and focused on her head. "I look amazing," she said out loud.

She really thought so.

She turned and considered her profile, the heart shape of her skull and its new veins, the exposed temple. "I honestly love it." She turned around and smiled hard, daring them to disagree.

"Me too," Ellie said, tentatively.

Who cared whether she meant it? In the grip of her new beauty, she wanted to be nice to Ellie now. Suddenly she saw them as two friends—sisters, really—united in their uncommon beauty.

"Yeah," said Rachel, playing with the hemp around her neck. "Definitely. Stunning."

Autry ducked under the doorframe and stepped into the bathroom. He palmed her head like a basketball, smiled, and said, "It's different."

"It makes my forehead wider, don't you think?"

"So wide you could park cars on it."

She was almost out of breath she was so pleased with this astonishing look that seemed to transform her, even her insides, into someone else.

"Very exotic," Autry went on. "I like my girls exotic."

Ellie was examining herself in the mirror now, her braid white with summer, strands unraveling around her face. "What about my forehead?" she asked.

And Chloe's old, overwhelming irritation for her returned. Why did she have to make everything about her?

"*Your* forehead," he said. "What about your forehead?" He smiled.

She turned to punch him in the abdomen, but he caught her wrists and they began to play-fight into the hallway. Rachel joined in.

Chloe turned back to the mirror.

The days bled into one another. Chloe woke up late—after Ellie, even. It was hard to fall asleep and hard to wake up in this kind of heat. She did her chores—mainly, she was in charge of washing clothes and keeping the house clean, because Rachel didn't like housework anymore.

They gardened in the heat. They went on with the Project as diligently as they could, she guessed, although she never saw Autry pick up a pen. Nobody was doing any writing, it seemed. She wasn't, anyway.

Still, Autry liked to regulate. He talked about what he *would* write, when he had time. They watched their trance meditation videos at night. They smoked weed. They played games to put themselves in trances by going: *We are one mind, one trance. We are one mind, one trance. We are one mind, one ever-deepening trance. We are one mind, one ever-deepening trance*—and, like that.

"Who's down for a hose-down?" Autry asked now, his arms around Ellie and Rachel.

"It's 'hose-down for a who's down,'" Rachel corrected.

Chloe looked at her. "What?"

"That's when you get hosed down and pretend to be someone else," Ellie explained, then fell into laughter with Rachel.

Chloe was sick to death of their puns and games and little jokes. Sometimes she resisted the urge to hate them. Sometimes she did actually hate them.

"It's a game they made up yesterday," Autry said, rubbing Chloe's head. "Come on. Before Ran gets here."

"You guys go." She wanted to be alone with her new head. She had to pee. Then she accidentally flushed.

They took official showers only once a week, but throughout the day they'd take turns holding the hose and standing in its cool jet. Lately the water was rust colored, and they didn't know why. But if she closed her eyes, it tasted regular.

They talked about calling a plumber, but didn't. "We don't really need random people over here all up in our shit," Autry concluded. He didn't even want his friends—the people he'd once invited—to come anymore.

Chloe studied her head from all angles. Behind her, through the mirror, was the open shower door with its frosted glass. A bar of soap in a metal holder hung from the neck of the showerhead. She couldn't see her head in the mirror now without seeing the shower, the showerhead.

She went to stand by the record player for a while. It was on, but there was no record turning. She liked to just wait beside it sometimes, to hear the occasional sound of frequency.

She couldn't remember where she'd heard that Edison had invented the phonograph to talk to dead people. But every time she walked past it, she stopped and listened. Sometimes it was the first thing she thought about when she woke up in the morning. Sometimes it was the showerhead.

She heard a line of static now. What did it *mean*? Was it decipherable, what were they saying?

She made herself pace around the house, picking clothes off the floor.

Outside, their voices, and the stream of the hose, reached her through the propped-open windows. Chloe understood now that she would never be one of them. But it didn't matter anymore, where it had mattered before.

The best she could explain it was this: When she looked at her things here—pillows propped on the headboard with its fracture down the middle, coffee cup with dregs of morning coffee, hemp necklaces on the vanity—she had the distinct feeling that it was all hers. Being here was her thing. She belonged. And when she did feel the occasional swirl of loneliness—now, for example—she went upstairs to think about her secrets.

· · ·

A month ago, they had finally met someone. A neighbor. The four of them (*One Year, Four People*) had gone swimming in the White River, cooling summer off their bodies. They lay on a rock while sun sparkled over the water like glass swept into a pile.

This guy, he was fishing on the bank across from them. Living out here, they rarely saw anyone. Sometimes the animals—the horses at the fence, the dogs and squirrels, the crickets in the dark, the chickens in the industrial chicken coop—seemed like the only other life.

Ellie waved.

He waved back.

His arms were dark red, his skinny chest pearl white. Soon he was wading through the shallow toward their rock. They had been reading passages out loud from *Not Buying It*. The author didn't buy anything but absolutely necessary consumables for a year. She lived off the junk already in her house.

When he approached, they all introduced themselves and exchanged the standard small talk about the weather and river. Ran said he grew up here, on his parents' small farm, a few miles away. He'd just turned twenty-one. They passed the weed around. When he quit coughing, he asked where they were from.

"You're from Fayetteville?" he said. "Ugh. I'm sorry."

"How so?" Ellie said, smiling.

"I hate cities. Those houses are so close together you could piss on all of them. The only thing good they got in Fayetteville is the strip clubs." He said that most of his friends were strippers.

Chloe, Ellie, and Rachel looked at each other and smiled.

They swam together from rock to rock, as the current

pressed against their thighs. They swam farther. They pulled themselves onto another rock.

Chloe had thought his name was Rand—short for *Randolph*, his given name. But on the first page of *Not Buying It* he wrote *Ran* beside his phone number.

They smoked more weed. He coughed. The weed he smoked was a different kind of weed, he said, he wasn't used to this kind.

Ran told stories about rescuing strippers—from ex-boyfriends, landlords, drugs, and the industry. He was Diamond and Angel's favorite customer. They would definitely hang out with him for free. If he wanted to, he said, he could.

Ran liked engines and Cormac McCarthy novels. He concocted special lip balm that he sold at farmers' markets. He didn't "get" college. He tried a semester at the University of Arkansas, but said it was a waste.

He had some business ventures of his own, but he helped his parents on their small farm. He loved his parents, it was clear, but he made them sound as helpless as possible.

He didn't ask many questions—other than where they were from, why they were here. It didn't seem to occur to him to ask questions. Their vague answers kept him talking about his own life. He'd bought himself a truck for his twenty-first birthday, and he talked about its engine.

He stared at Ellie's white bikini top when he talked. When he told stories about strippers though, he looked as far as possible into the horizon. Just as they were getting tired of him, he said he had work to do, and went away.

But he'd showed up the next day, at the house, with a

cooler of trout he'd caught and a cardboard box of fresh cantaloupe, peaches, and jars of honey.

Ellie and Rachel met him at his truck, while Chloe stood beside Autry and watched from the open window.

"Holy shit," Ran exclaimed, stepping down from his truck. "You need to mow your lawn."

"Oh," Rachel said, waving her hand. "No."

"What do you mean, no? What are all the flags for? Do you *have* a mower? If you need one, I could sell one of mine for forty bucks," he offered.

"We have one, it might work, I don't know, but what's the point? The amount of carbon dioxide emitted from mowing your lawn is, like, four times the amount of carbon naturally collected and stored by the lawn itself."

"Huh? How long have you lived here?"

"Then it just grows back," Rachel continued. "I mean, what's the point, seriously?"

"Don't get me wrong," Ran said. "Show me around."

Autry and Chloe met them on the back deck, and they all walked around the yard, then to the creek, where gnats floated over the green-tinted surface of the water. It was hot and overcast. Sweat beaded everyone's noses. They walked back, passing the row of berry bushes. Ran picked a few, then threw one into the air, and caught it in his mouth.

"Those are poisonous," Ellie said. "Aren't they?"

"These?" A high-pitched laugh escaped Ran. "These aren't poisonous!" He laughed again. "Why—did you think they were poisonous?"

"No," Ellie insisted, and gave him a push. She winked at Rachel. "I was just kidding."

He gave her a little push back. Then he looked afraid. "Did I hurt you?"

"What?"

"I didn't hurt you, did I? Sometimes I forget how strong I am. It happens. I just have this thing—I don't hurt women. I'm just wired that way." He bent down and picked a weed. "That's just me."

"What did that weed ever do to you?" Autry asked.

Ran gave him a strange look.

When they completed the loop back into the driveway, Ran said, "What's up with these cars?" He touched Autry's Tacoma, the fogged-over window of the camper. "This an '04?"

Autry scratched his head. "Uh . . . yeah. Maybe an '05."

Ran squatted to his knees, beside one of the tires. "No, it's an '04. Just not running? I can take a look at it."

"That's all right, we've got—" Autry nodded his head toward Chloe's Camry.

"What's wrong with that one?" he asked, eyes trained on Ellie's Honda.

"Timing belt–related issues," Ellie said.

As they tried to make their way back inside, Ran pressed his foot on a soft deck board over and over. "You're going to need to do something about this. Shit. And soon. I could replace your deck if you needed me to. I can probably get to it next week. I mean, I can cut the boards, and I could do it—"

"Let's eat, huh?" Autry exclaimed. "I'm starving."

Rachel grilled the fish and steamed the vegetables, and Autry cut some fruit into pieces the way they do in the grocery store. They were quiet through dinner. Ran mentioned that she had overcooked the fish. "Most people do," he said. She stared back at him. Nobody seemed to be in a particularly good mood except for Ran, who talked and talked.

They didn't know what to do with him after dinner, so they smoked weed on the deck while the night brought its chorus of invisible insects. Autry played "The Swimming Song" on his guitar. They were all stoned.

This summer I swam in the ocean
And I swam in a swimming pool
Salt my wounds, chlorine my eyes
I'm a self-destructive fool, I'm a self-destructive fool.

Before Ran left, he asked if they had enough wood for the winter. "Best to get it now," he said.

They looked at each other.

"I'll bring you some next time I'm out here," he said, when they didn't respond.

This morning, when Chloe still had a head of hair, Ran called and asked if he could come over. Rachel had answered the phone, and Autry was vehemently shaking his head. But Rachel said, "Sure. Tonight, you mean?"

When Rachel hung up, Autry raised his arms. "Why?"

"Because," she replied, "he might bring us some free stuff. Stuff we like, need. Like food."

"We have plenty of food." This was true. But everything was drying up in the garden. They'd managed even to let the zucchini go, which Chloe thought was supposed to be indestructible.

When Chloe came back downstairs for dinner, Ran was there, just as he said he'd be. He was standing over the stove with a spatula in his hand, wearing Lee jeans stuffed into white tennis shoes, and a collared shirt that said NAUTICA. His cologne was overwhelming. "Hello, Chloe," he said, and made a mock-gesture of an elaborate bow.

"See what I did to my hair?" Chloe said.

"I got eyes—what the hell happened?"

Chloe smiled; she didn't care what he thought.

"Can I feel it?"

She proudly tilted her head toward him, into the steam from the stove top rising toward the light bulb. "Smooth as a baby's head," he said.

Ellie was sitting on the countertop beside the stove, mindlessly tapping her bare heels against the cabinet beneath her, telling him jokes. She was wearing tiny white shorts that made her legs long and dark.

Ran, naturally, was infatuated with her. She tortured him by flirting with him, ignoring him, and flirting with him again—until he was paralyzed with devotion.

"Taste this," Ran said, holding a piece of fish on his finger. "It's my own seasoning—it's good, right?"

Chloe tasted it. It was incredibly good. The salt on his finger made her lips sting.

Ellie said, "Can I taste?"

"Of course, my lady."

"Did you bring any more lip balm?" Chloe asked.

He reached into his pocket and handed her a clear tube of his lip balm.

"And does Autry still owe you money for stuff, by the way?" Chloe whispered.

Ran looked at Autry. He was in the great room reading to Rachel, who was twisted in a stretch for her back.

"Yeah," Ran whispered. "He does. But don't worry about it."

"Sorry."

"I think you guys need it more than me," Ran said, smiling.

Chloe could not live without Ran's homemade lip balm of beeswax and sunflower oils. "It's doing well at the farmers' markets," he said. "It's weird, you know, I've been making it practically all my life. Suddenly everyone wants it. I've got all these orders for it."

Rachel and Ellie went outside to set the wrought-iron table. Through the glass doors, Chloe watched their dialogue of hips and arms. She watched their mouths laugh, their teeth like pretty rows of shells.

Chloe took the bowl of potato salad, made with yogurt and dill, to the table. The night was heady and thick with late summer. A few stars blinked on and off in the sky, and something about the night especially brought the cicadas. Ran told them everything he knew about cicadas. It was coming to the end of their seventeen-year cycle, he said, and they would be louder than anything then.

Chloe couldn't imagine numbering another summer. It

was hard to see even past tomorrow here. She could not imagine watching another year repeat its days.

After two stabs at her fish and a piece of fruit that made her tongue rough like a cat's tongue, her stomach was full of pins. They disappeared only when she quit eating and lay flat on her back.

She couldn't eat very much at all lately; she'd lost more weight. "I'm full," she said, pushing away her plate. "It was amazing though."

"Did you not like it?" Rachel asked.

"Try the potato salad," Ellie added.

"I'm just full." Could she be more clear?

Ran reached over and put his fork into her fish.

"Take the plate," she said, gratefully.

She wondered if the pain had to do with eating meat and dairy again. When Ran came, he always brought fish or meat. He could tell you the life and death of the animal; it was okay to eat meat then.

Autry said her stomach hurt because she was releasing the toxins of her previous unhealth. He called it "Doing Battle with the Old World." On the upside, not being able to eat coincided perfectly with a small unwritten rule of the house: Don't eat very much (eat responsibly), but act stuffed all the time.

She felt certain her meal of vitamins from the Old World would help. She could ask Ran to buy them, on one of his trips to Platinum and the Silver Dollar, or one of his trips to sell pottery and lip balm at farmers' markets in Fayetteville and Bentonville. But then, they came in all that packaging, and the idea of swallowing strange pills should be devastating. She went inside and lay on the floor of the great room, trying to free her stomach muscles with her mind.

She opened another book she was supposed to be reading, called *The Art of Dumpster Diving.* She opened it to a chapter called "Clean Up After Yourself." *If you've thrown garbage all around, pick it up and put it back into the dumpster. While you're at it, throw away other nearby trash that's on the ground. Leave the area as clean or cleaner than you found it. Don't give dumpster diving a bad name.*

Next chapter: "Networking with Other Divers."

Ran left after dinner. As usual, they felt relieved and guilty. Autry hated him, but tried to hide it, unsuccessfully. "He's just around too much," Autry said.

Chloe thought he was fine, just young—but competent. He made Autry seem *in*competent. But that was okay, because she thought she was pretty competent herself. She did know how to bake sourdough now. She washed clothes, didn't she? She was able to quit pulling out her hair, as of today. Pretty soon, Jim would be here and they'd be together. Jim was the secret she kept locked up inside her. No one could know. Her secret kept her whole, it kept everything else shut out. Perhaps they'd get married.

The four of them sat Indian-style on the floor and smoked some weed, trying to forget about Ran. Ellie passed her turns; Rachel took double hits.

Autry came back from the bathroom and said, disappointed, "Chloe . . . you flushed."

"I know. I'm so sorry. I forgot."

They talked about the Project. Soon, Autry said, he would be drafting the first chapter. Soon. But first he needed more research on their previous lives of unhealth.

"The plan is, for the first part of the book, I'm thinking a sort of profile of each of us, like personal histories," he said. "We could have these accounts of where we started, and the book could show where we finished. You know— our journey from unhealth to health. Beginning with the unhealth of the Old World. A breaking point would be good. I want to call the chapter 'Personal Histories of Unhealth.' We could start by talking after dinner tomorrow night, whenever. I mean, everyone's had unhealth in their lives, it's part of being human in the Old World. So think about some defining moments of unhealth in your life."

"I was raped," Ellie offered.

"Really?" Autry said. "That's fantastic."

"I mean, it was confusing. Never mind."

"No, no—rape is perfect. More stuff like that."

"I don't know if I was. Consent is weird."

"Oh, you were raped all right."

They passed the lighter and bowl around again, and then they looked at their collection of CDs with TRANSCEND written on the faces of the discs. Autry waved a few in his hand like tickets.

"Brain orgasms. What do we want tonight? How about an assortment of tingling sounds by Whispering Pines, or a fake tattoo consultation by Heather Feather?"

They discussed the pros and cons, then decided on the fake tattoo consultation.

"I just never knew that this was an actual *thing*," Ellie

said, for the millionth time. "I can't get over it. I used to *always* watch QVC in my apartment in Fayetteville. I loved hearing the women discuss jewelry, it was so soothing. It was like getting a massage, but a brain massage. I just didn't know it was a real thing that people set out to do."

Did she honestly not remember saying this every time, Chloe wondered, or was it simply imperative to clarify that she'd been doing this kind of trance meditation long before them? In *her* mind, probably before anyone in the world.

"I heard some people calling it ASMR, but it's not official yet or anything. Scientists don't even know," Autry said.

"What does *ASMR* stand for though?" Ellie asked.

"Autonomous sensory meridian response."

"Meaning . . ."

"Like, auditory-tactile synesthesia."

"Let's just go with it's a euphoric experience," Rachel said. "A combination of positive feelings, personal attention, relaxation . . ."

"And the amazing head tingling," Chloe added.

Autry opened his Mac, tilting the screen so the image darkened then lightened into focus.

Heather Feather, a young woman with dark hair and soothing eyes, entered and began to whisper. "*Did you doze off waiting for me?*" She spoke softly, like a pretty child. "*You're here for a new tattoo, I see. Do you know what you may want to get?*" She paused. "*No? Well, it's not the first time I've had someone come in needing a little guidance. I have a portfolio I'm going to show you, just different things that I do.*"

For the next hour, Heather Feather took care of them, she

made decisions, she showed them image after image of tattoos until it was mind-numbing. Heather Feather was God.

Heather Feather tapped her fingernails against the desk. She drew in her sketchbook, for the sound of charcoal marking the page again and again. She turned the plastic pages of her binder slowly. The pleasure was crippling. Chloe's head tingled with little bubbles, like someone had just cracked open her skull and poured champagne on the neurons.

When the house was dark and blanketed in sleep, Chloe eased out of bed and stepped back into her cutoffs, the denim still let-go and warm with her body, like putting her skin back on.

Stitched vertically down the zipper's inside fabric were the words LUCKY YOU. Every time she pulled the zipper and worked the button she wondered—was this supposed to be ironic, or sexy?

"Sexy," Ellie said the other day. "The words are upside down, so it's meant for someone else." Ellie, the expert. "Like, that person is lucky because they're unzipping your jeans. It's dumb, but that's what it means."

"Look, it's printed backwards to you, so it's for someone else to see," Rachel agreed.

Still, Chloe leaned toward the ironic: LUCKY YOU, a little sinister, the letters themselves winking at her every morning as she put clothes on to face the day.

She could hear Ellie turning in her sleep across the hall. When the air stilled again, Chloe walked like a sleepwalker down the steps and into the kitchen. Rachel and Autry slept with a shut door. Chloe never knew if they could hear her going up and down the steps every night.

She felt her way through the darkness, touching the walls, the table, and finally the phone in its cradle. She tiptoed back upstairs with the phone over her chest.

If she didn't call *him*, they wouldn't talk. She didn't care. She'd keep calling him every night, relentlessly. Jim needed to be shown how the world existed for him. She knew this for sure, after the second time she saw Crush Heat Burn at Natalie's, in May, when she'd come with his phone in her pocket, and the band crashed with her for the second time. She told him he was amazing, repeatedly.

They all went to brunch the next day. They got a little stupid off pitcher-mimosas, and afterward, she and Jim slept all afternoon in bed with the sound of the fan going. They stayed in bed for a week, sleeping and having sex, in and out of wakefulness.

Chloe believed in her bones that he was not in love with Ellie—may never have been—but the occasional troubling thoughts still surfaced.

She climbed out from her window, onto the roof that slanted toward the faded wildflowers that appeared brushed into the grass, as in a painting. She dialed his number by heart, and he finally picked up, sounding sleepy, or in the middle of something.

She could hear air—motion—as though he were walking.

"Hey," she said. "What are you up to?"

"Just sitting here. You?"

"It's hot and everyone's asleep. I shaved my head. Ran

came over. How was your show tonight? Or did you guys just practice?"

"We played at the Hole in the Wall. Wait—you shaved your head?"

"I wanted to text you a picture. But . . . I can't of course . . . the Internet and cell phone situation . . ."

"Just, wow. I'd rather see this in person." He laughed. "Will it grow back before I see you in November?"

"I'm just going to keep it bald."

"Hot." He laughed a little. "I thought nobody liked Ran?"

"Well, he's sweet, and helpful, and just—well, he's just innocent, but wants to give the impression of having been around. He's smart about some stuff though. Like survival, I guess."

In November Jim was doing a tour in Northwest Arkansas and Missouri, and he said he wanted to visit Autry. It was *her* he was visiting—not Autry. She knew this. But whatever his reasons were—fear, self-protection?—he needed to phrase it this way. She played along. "Autry will be really glad to see you."

But Autry was so wrapped up with the Project, and health, that Chloe wasn't at all sure how he'd react to someone dropping by, even someone he'd once invited.

Rachel said that all men, even Autry's friends, were intimidated by him. Chloe doubted it. Chloe liked Autry, even though sometimes she thought he was full of shit.

"How does he like being the only man in a house with three women?" Jim asked.

"I think he likes it."

"I bet he does."

"Are you still going to Harvest Fest next week?"

"Yeah. You should come to Harvest, and camp with some of your buddies. You'd like it, it's a gorgeous spot right on top of the mountain."

"I love music festivals," she said. She'd never been to one. "But they need me here. I'm really a big part of things here."

"I don't know how long I can stay, when I come see Autry. I don't know how long I can hack it."

"Oh, you'd be surprised how long you could stay."

"My buddy Dane's got this girl who shows up all the time now."

"What is she like?"

"I don't know, cute, I guess, if you like what she's selling, you know, makeup and high heels. They make a great . . . team," he said, and Chloe laughed. "She works at Dillard's. We stay with her sometimes."

"Dillard's." The word sounded familiar, but it belonged to another world. The Old World. "Dillard's." When it finally registered, she laughed. "Oh, *Dillard's*—like the department store in the mall."

Suddenly there was something altogether hilarious about Dillard's and the world of Dillard's.

"Something funny?" He laughed. "When was the last time you were in Dillard's?"

"Seventh grade. I stole a pair of jeans. I put them in my backpack in the dressing room."

"From Dillard's?"

"From Dillard's." She laughed again. It felt great to laugh— she wanted to prolong the laughter.

She looked down. Her fingers were wet. She'd been scratching her bites without realizing it, and now blood was smeared around senselessly like finger paint. "Oh. I'm bleeding. It's going to make them swarm. I should go."

"Make who swarm?"

"The mosquitoes. I scratched my bites."

"You should put some cream on those bites."

"No, that stuff is so toxic." Something about the way he said *cream* was really sexy, however.

"You sure it's cool if I come stay with you?"

She smiled into the receiver. "Positive."

"How do you think Ellie's going to handle it?"

"Don't worry about Ellie. Ellie's fine." Were people ever going to stop worrying over her?

"I'll see you soon then," he said. "My buddy here in Austin that I've been staying with in his little house, well, his girlfriend is moving in. I need a place to crash. I want to write some songs, too. But I'm broke as fuck."

When she hung up, her ears rang with happiness. She loved how he always warmed up by the end.

She had to just keep getting him so used to these calls that he started relying on them. She leaned back and regarded the sky, its black theater of stars. The whole galaxy belonged to her, and she belonged to it.

• • •

She woke up to the sound of Rachel playing tennis against the side of the house. The ball went back and forth between her racquet and the wall like music beats.

It was hard coming alive again in this kind of heat. All

night Chloe struggled on the verge of sleep and daydream, feeling for the cool places on the sheet. Instead of sleeping, or fully waking up, she lived in a realm of chronic drowsiness, in which the frequency of the record player and silence of the showerhead beat the circuit of her thoughts.

She lay there for a while, she didn't know how long, thinking of her mother. She could stay in bed forever. If she never got up again, that would be okay with her.

"It's my *exercise*," she heard Rachel saying.

Chloe lifted her head now, to listen. Rachel had stormed inside from playing tennis, apparently, and now she was at the bottom of the stairs.

"Don't be jealous of a tennis racquet. I'm just—working out."

"Working out? We don't 'work out' here."

"I'm still into the Project, Autry—I swear. I am. I am."

"Do we need to get you a gym membership, baby—some of those Nike running shorts the college girls wear? You want to go back to the tanning bed? And another thing—I don't want Ran over here anymore. I want him gone."

Rachel dropped her racquet on the floor.

But by the time Chloe came down for breakfast, they were at peace again. Rachel was feeding him a piece of fruit with her fingers.

Chloe bit into a tomato. Her stomach began, immediately, to hurt. She put it back on the shelf in the refrigerator, and went upstairs again. Did her stomach really hurt, she wondered, or was it just the voices in her head—her thoughts—telling her that her stomach hurt? Was there a difference?

She tied on a bathing suit from the wardrobe of bikinis strewn everywhere, then covered her head with a silk scarf, tying a little knot under her neck, the way her mother used to wear scarves.

Ellie knocked on her half-open door. This was irritating, because nobody knocked on doors. "Come in," Chloe said, stepping into her LUCKY YOUs. The knocking continued. "Come *in*."

"Oh," Ellie said, stepping inside. "Can I borrow a pair of cutoffs?"

"What?"

"Can I borrow—"

"But you don't have to ask. They're not mine . . . they're everyone's."

"I just thought, since you're doing laundry today—I didn't want to wear something you wanted to wash."

"Wear whatever you want."

Ellie picked up a pair—the pair Chloe now wanted desperately to wear.

"I don't mean to be confrontational or whatever. Have I done something to you?" Ellie said.

"Why would I be mad at you?"

"That's what I'm asking you."

When Chloe didn't respond, Ellie said, "Why do you hate me? I'm tired of this constant attack."

Chloe still didn't respond.

"Never mind. Why bother," Ellie said, and started to walk out of the room.

"Wait," Chloe said, half wanting to apologize.

Ellie turned around and stood there.

But for what was she supposed to apologize? Things were just tangled up; there were ropes around them; there was nothing to say.

"What are those?" Ellie asked.

"What are what?"

Chloe followed the line of Ellie's gaze. Ellie was looking at Phoenix's cowboy boots. They were under her bed, the red toes sticking out.

"Where did you get those boots?" Ellie asked.

"Oh. At a show."

"A show?"

"Phoenix . . . Pace gave them to me." Chloe felt this wasn't a total lie. They *were* his boots, even if she'd bought them.

Ellie's expression went flat with rage, and her voice cracked when she started to talk. "A Crush Heat Burn show?"

"It's kind of a long story," Chloe said. Her heart was beating fast.

Ellie stood there for a beat, eyes burning. "You need to get a life—your own." She turned around and walked down the stairs.

• • •

Chloe stood by the record player for a while, listening for the frequency, then went outside with the laundry. She had her own life, didn't she? She had Jim, didn't she? She was here, a member of the Project, wasn't she? The day was hot and damp, with a wall of clouds in all corners of the sky. They'd probably get a storm later.

She liked how she paid attention to weather now. It was its own thing—it mattered. It wasn't like in the Old World, when she'd walk out blankly into the day, as if it were owed to her.

Chloe also marveled at once using machines for the simple task of washing clothes—as if washing machines were magical. As if it were some mysterious and complicated process. Rinse, wash, agitate, rinse, repeat—where was the mystery?

And dryers. Dryers, especially—what a waste.

She liked doing laundry. She'd always liked repetitive jobs where it was easy to drift. Rolling flatware at Viceroy, for example, was a thing she preferred.

Chloe put away the washboard, the extra bins with soap bubbles still drying in rainbows at the bottom. She hung the clothes to dry on the clothesline that crossed between two trees. She'd wanted Ellie to see the boots, but she didn't know why. What did she expect to happen?

Rachel helped her hang clothes. They used Chloe's old barrettes for pins—something Ellie never would have thought of, because she wasn't a true conservationist. She wasn't serious about the rules. She was just killing time. Chloe did care about the planet, she told herself—didn't she?—as she pinned the waists of the cutoffs to the line, making a row of invisible people.

"Hey, Rachel," Chloe called out. "Remember Dillard's?"

Rachel looked up from beneath her khaki-colored sun hat. For the first time, Chloe noticed how a sunspot had darkened under her right eye.

"Dillard's? Why?"

"Nothing." Chloe smiled. "I was just thinking about that store."

"God. Malls."

"It's kind of funny, isn't it?"

"No, it's not funny. I can't even wrap my head around a dead mall right now. Why would you even bring up the Old World?"

The word *Dillard's* repeated in her head. *Dillard's, Dillard's, Dillard's, Dillard's*—until the meaning of the word began to come apart. She liked getting lost in words like that, until they didn't mean anything. *Dillard's Dillard's Dillard's Dillard's Dillard's.*

Rachel walked away with the empty laundry basket on her hip while Chloe sat down in the grass, with the four-leaf clovers, and watched the clothes stir under the hot gray sun. Her face was tight from smiling—but it was a strained kind of smile, a plastered smile, as if screwed on.

She got up and walked inside the house. She undressed in the bathroom, taking off the heat of the day. Even so, she turned the shower faucet to hot. An egg timer sat on the counter because showers were to last no more than five minutes in cold water.

But she didn't use the timer now.

Sometime long after she got in, there was a knock at the door.

It was like the tapping of the razor against the glass bowl of water, when they were shaving her head. *Listen.*

"Chloe?"

Rachel said her name again.

"Chloe—why is it so hot in here?" She opened the shower curtain.

"Leave me alone," Chloe said. She wanted to concentrate.

She wanted her mother. She stood there under the stream of water, staring into the showerhead, thinking of her gold rings and silk scarves.

"Leave me alone," she said again, although she didn't know if Rachel was still there.

She desperately wanted to hear something—something that mattered. *The quieter you become, the more you can hear.* She kept staring at the showerhead. DELTA was etched between the little dots, the speakers, where streams of water came out. She stood still, staring into the showerhead. Eventually, the water turned cold. Eventually, everything went quiet except the noise inside her own head, which was growing louder.

SEXY/IRONIC

ELLIE

The BioLife Plasma donation center was fluorescent as a hospital, turning everyone shades of sea green. A glare moved along the floor, in between the row of beige chairs that looked like dentist chairs. Ellie lay in one, her right arm extended for the tech. He kept missing her vein, until he found what he called a side vein. He told her to make a fist, to pump.

The lettering of his T-shirt bled through his thin lab coat, and his wrists were tattooed with dragons and comic book figures and the death dates of his friends. He balled paper towels for her to squeeze. The needle would go straight through if she didn't keep her arm straight. This had the perverse effect of making her want to bend her arm. He marked his clipboard and moved on.

She coughed and the needle vibrated in her skin. She pumped again until the *beep*, then relaxed while the plasma separated, and the blood drained back inside.

Tubes of blood and plasma ran across her lap into the bag at her hip. She liked watching the drip. Everywhere she looked, people sat attached to these bags of their insides, the stuff that made them, filling up the plastic. They sat in positions of discomfort. Their discomfort seemed not so much from donating plasma though as from the circumstances that brought them here.

Ellie looked at them. One man with pale skin and a red beard looked back. He was wearing a Harvest Fest sweatshirt, and though she couldn't make out its list of bands written in colored fonts, she knew CRUSH HEAT BURN was somewhere on his chest.

The whole thing took about forty minutes. Then there was the saline injection; its chemistry made her freeze.

She signed out with her finger, the red laser scanning her print. Thirty dollars was added to her orange-issue BioLife debit card, and she walked out into the teeth of November.

It was Election Day.

She wasn't voting. She wasn't registered. On the sidewalk,

a woman hurried by with a white sticker on her jacket: I VOTED. Somehow everyone was getting all this voting done.

Ran had voted that morning at a little brick church. Autry and Rachel voted absentee, they said. But when Ellie asked where they picked up the forms, Rachel was vague. "You know, at the absentee voter registry."

"Oh."

"Bureau," Rachel added.

Chloe wasn't voting because Chloe refused to get out of bed. "Chloe has lost her sense of balance here," Autry explained.

Chloe said that her stomach hurt. "Like knives," she said. She couldn't eat. All day she lay in bed, making sounds of pain, with her hands balled together at her chest and a T-shirt over her eyes. She talked about her mother without making any sense. When she did get out of bed, she spent time in the shower, standing there in all her clothes, without turning the water on, staring at the showerhead. When they asked what she was doing, she'd get defensive. "Nothing," she said. "Why?"

Ellie waited at the crosswalk, holding the hood of her sweatshirt around her face. Cars rushed back and forth while a plastic bag with plastic bags inside it tumbled over the median.

Que Sera seemed asleep behind its big black window, the corner of a shopping center. Ellie walked inside and found it half empty. Chinese lanterns hung from the ceiling and smoke stuck to the air, although all the bars in Fayetteville had just turned smoke-free.

She ordered the special: a shot and a beer for $4.50. Rail whiskey and PBR. Some out-of-towners wandered in, thinking Que Sera was a Mexican restaurant. They wanted tacos. When they saw what it really was—a dive bar with dive bar food—they walked back out, bewildered.

She slid her orange BioLife card across the bar. Plasma is ninety percent water, so the whiskey went straight to her heart. Through the window, she saw Michael Lindsey pulling into the lot, right on time.

She turned to study her image in the mirror of liquor bottles, her collarbone a pale shelf between the zipper of her sweatshirt. Her eyes were ringed with purple shadows.

She pushed her hair behind her ear. Once, she felt beautiful. Now, she just felt like herself.

Michael stood in the parking lot beside his black car, talking on the phone, using gestures with his free hand as though the other person were there. The man with the Harvest Fest sweatshirt approached from a truck. He nodded to Michael before walking inside Que Sera, but Michael didn't notice him.

The man ordered the special. People on the edge went to BioLife for thirty dollars and the bonus of dehydration. They got drunk faster. She and the man traded head nods, in the spirit of two people doing shots in the middle of a Tuesday. He carried his beer to the iJuke and touched a Neil Young song on the selector. The machine's play of colors washed over his face. "Heart of Gold." There was a time, she thought. There was a time when she would have slept with him, so easy. This not only seemed obscene now, but boring. Sex—it was so monotonous when you thought about it.

She was numb from the saline, numb inside her jeans. LUCKY YOU was starting to feel ironic, after all, not sexy.

The door closed behind Michael. He brought the cold inside with him. When they hugged, she felt the beginning of winter in his coat. They sat in a dark corner booth. He looked younger and more handsome here, in real life, than in the image that revolved in her head all day. Sitting across from him now, she was unable to speak.

He sighed. "Well. Here we are," he said, looking around.

She nodded and drank.

"You called *me*, remember?"

She coughed into her elbow and said, "Why are you acting weird?"

"Why am *I* acting weird? I just drove by BioLife Plasma and saw you standing in some dirty clothes a few minutes ago."

"These clothes?" She looked down at her clothes. These clothes weren't dirty—they'd gone through Chloe's last wash cycle, after all. "You think just because they're not brand-new . . ."

"Honey, you'll never convert me to whatever it is you do out there in the hills. Let's be clear about that right now. But don't donate plasma. I would rather just give you the money."

"Really? It's temporary."

He picked up the empty shot glass and looked through it, then picked up the beer can, too. "For this?"

"Michael, it's a beer. Not heroin."

"Have you talked to your parents?"

"I call them every now and then, and tell them I'm fine. I mean, I may as well have come out of a vending machine."

"Promise me that if you ever need money, you'll ask me. Doesn't it feel wrong to sell off your body?"

"Sell off my body!" She laughed. "Michael, people need plasma."

"If other people need plasma, don't you think you need plasma?"

"I'm healthier than I've ever been."

"Oh, right," he said. "You're the picture of health."

She drank. "How's Marianne?"

"She's fine."

"Still the picture of health?"

That was mean, and she apologized.

He said it was okay.

"She lost the baby a couple weeks ago."

"Baby?"

"Second trimester."

"Wait—baby?"

He looked away, then looked back. "I thought you may have known that she was pregnant."

"How would I know that?"

He shrugged. "She has an eating disorder, too. That's how she lost the baby. Anyway, we'll try again."

The figure from the parking deck restroom reappeared, the blond head tilted toward the mirror. *You're an ugly little girl, aren't you?* Ellie imagined her throwing up a bloody fetus in the toilet. "Did she have an eating disorder before she married you?"

"Don't be cruel."

"I'm sorry. I'm happy to see you, and this is how I'm handling it."

"Right. I didn't forget how you treat your boyfriends."

"'Boyfriend' . . . please. It was so confusing when I saw you. I don't know."

She slouched back in her chair, and he moved his knee between her knees.

"Want to hear something depressing?" he asked.

"Of course."

"So we're in couple's therapy the other day, right? And Marianne's talking about this, this—this eating disorder thing. I hate the word *bulimia*, I'm not going to use it."

"Wait." She turned toward the passing waitress. "Can I order some food?" She glanced at the menu. "It just reminded me. Sorry. Cheese fries," she told the waitress, then ordered another shot and beer. Michael ordered an iced tea.

Sometimes she felt as if she were swallowing rocks, but the Old Crow soothed her throat. Since she'd started donating plasma, she kept this cough. Her nose ran and she was generally out of breath.

"Anyway, Marianne says that what she really likes is to taste the food again—like ice cream and Dr Pepper. She likes how it tastes when they come back up. Cereal, Rice Krispies, and so forth. She says she honestly thinks it tastes better coming up. Can you think of anything more depressing than that?"

She thought for a moment. "Yes, I can. But I think you should try to think of the whole miscarriage thing as a blessing."

"What?"

"Very recently a man in Little Rock was crushed in his apartment's trash compactor. He was looking for his phone, which he had dropped down the chute by accident—"

"That's not what I meant," he said. "I meant, what the fuck do you mean the miscarriage is a blessing? I want a child."

"You want a child? With your wife?"

"I want a child."

"Imposing life on someone is the ultimate crime."

"Come on."

"We're overpopulating the earth. Fifty babies are born every second, did you know that? If everyone just quit having babies, then maybe the earth's biosphere could return to normal." She paused. "If we phase out the human race, the earth could breathe again."

"Oh, good lord." He stared at her. "You don't actually believe this stuff you're saying, do you?"

That was beside the point. "I'm stating the simple fact that we'd be better off with less people," she said.

"So why don't your friends just kill themselves?"

"Maybe we will. The world's going to end in 2012, anyway."

"What about donating plasma? You know you're saving lives, right?"

"I'm not saving anyone's life, probably. I mean, who knows what they actually do with that stuff. I probably shouldn't though, you're right, Autry would be mad."

"Who's Autry?"

"Only my friend Ran knows."

"Who's Rand? Who are these people?"

"Nobody."

They ate cheese fries. Michael put a few on his plate, then tipped the ranch to one side, while Ellie grabbed from the platter.

"You realize," Michael said, "that everything you say about what—'health'?—and everything you're reading, or pretending to read, and what you're doing out there, is a fucking cliché, right? It's so trite, honey—"

"So?" The fries and the cheese and the bacon were getting the tips of her fingers wet and greasy. She didn't care.

"So, you're not a trite person. I don't . . . *like* where you live. I don't like that you left without telling me. Why did you leave like that?"

"How do you know where I live?"

"Because. It's 2008. Nobody just . . . disappears."

"Well, but."

"Well nothing. They don't. I saw you last week, you know, but that wasn't the first time I saw you. The first time I saw you, I was driving by and you were walking out of this bar, and you got into a truck with someone—Rand? Is that supposed to be Rand?"

"Ran."

"Right, so then I followed you back to your place."

She was touched, but she couldn't let him know it. "You followed me?"

"Of course—"

"Oh, no. Don't look now, but there's this woman I used to know. Don't look now."

He twisted around and looked at her anyway.

Now Lorraine was walking over, saying, "Ellie?"

Ellie raised her head. "Oh, hey."

Lorraine was wearing a black sweater with a little white I VOTED sticker on her boob. Her hair was swept-up; she looked pretty. "What are you doing here? We didn't know you were still in town."

"Oh, I'm not. I'm just sort of visiting. You know, to vote."

"Is this your boyfriend?" She smiled at Michael.

Michael smiled back.

Ellie looked to Michael for help.

"Michael Lindsay," he said, offering his hand. "Pleased to meet you."

Ellie drank through a silence.

"Well, just how are you?" Lorraine said.

"Good. So, um, what are you doing here? How's Viceroy?"

"Good, business is good. Just borrowing some linens for a party. You've still got a paycheck at Viceroy, you know. Your tip-out from the last week you worked. We would have mailed it to you, but we didn't know where, we didn't have an address . . ."

"Oh, don't worry about it."

Lorraine said that it was good to see her, to take care, and smiled at Michael as she walked away behind the bar.

"She's nice," Michael said.

"That was acting. She wanted to fire me. Anyway, people *do* disappear. I disappeared. I don't know where, but . . . I don't know what I'm saying. Whatever, god. Did you vote today?"

"Yes. I voted."

"And?"

"And I'm not telling you how I voted."

"Then I know how you voted."

"It's not a crime to vote Republican."

"It should be a crime to vote for Sarah Palin."

"Let me get you out of that place."

"No, I can't leave Rachel there. I told her I'd stay until June. That will be one year. After that . . . I don't know. But I know that I will not leave Rachel there. And anyway, what would you even do? You're married. You want babies."

"You could work for me again, doing . . . doing whatever. We could get you another apartment. I could move you in, and you'll get all settled, and I could come over like once a week."

"Once a week . . ." Something about this hurt her deeply, but it was confusing; she didn't know why. Regardless, she couldn't let him know. He was only someone who had once given her a job, she reminded herself. Nothing more. She stared at him.

She wanted him to talk about a future, like he used to, when she knew that he loved her for sure. She couldn't stop herself: "But . . . do you still love me?"

"Of course I love you. Would I be sitting here?"

"Why?"

"Why do I love you? You really want to know?"

She nodded.

He paused. "You're the only person who can make me feel insecure."

She thought about this; it was something.

"Now. But the real question. Do you love *me*?"

"God, no. Why would you ask me that?" She drank her beer so that he wouldn't see if she ended up smiling.

He held her wrist across the table. "Promise me you'll stop self-destructing, Ellie."

"I'm *not* self-destructing. I'm healthy. I didn't drink for three whole months, so don't give me your morals and bull-shit." She took her hand away. "I could go without drinking again—anytime—but why? Why should I? Why am I not drunk all the time? Why isn't everyone? Why are we all not out on the streets, constantly drinking?"

He took her hand again, and put it to his lips. "Don't talk like that."

"Did you and Marianne go to Jackson Hole this summer?" she asked softly. "For vacation, in August?"

"Why do you ask?"

"So you did. Did you have a good time?"

"Not particularly."

"Is that where Marianne got pregnant?"

"Where is this coming from?"

Tears filled her eyes; she looked away. What was wrong with her?

"Not jealous, are you?" He smiled. His eyes softened when she didn't say anything. "No. Look—we went to this great jazz show one night. I mean, phenomenal jazz. We ate, we drank—I thought we were having a good time, by our standards. We get back home and she goes, 'I *hate* the saxophone.'"

"Really?"

"Then she slept in the guest room."

She turned her head at the movement outside, in the parking lot. Ran was pulling his truck into a space. The visor was low, even though there was no sun. "I have to go," she said. She put the beer to her lips and drained it.

She relaxed her purse across her shoulder and brushed a strand of hair from her eyes. She stood up. "Don't walk me out."

He left money on the table, put his coat on, and walked her out anyway. "See me next week," he was saying, as they made it to the door.

"I want to. It depends."

"On what does it depend?" They were standing outside the black glass-front now. Ran waited with one hand at the wheel, the motor running.

"I guess this is where we part ways," she said. She moved to go, but he held on to her hand. "I go / you stay; / two autumns," she said. "That's a haiku."

"Don't disappear again."

"But I thought nobody just disappeared."

She felt his smile, and she smiled.

He let go. "Be good, Ellie."

She got into Ran's truck and clicked the seatbelt over her lap. They took off and eased into the traffic that tightened onto the road in two strict lanes. Easy chords of top-forty country played on the radio. She was relieved not to be alone, trapped with the confusion of her Michael-feelings.

The days of aloneness, of walking through the dregs of the seasons to the state of her apartment, were over. She did not have to consider her neighbor's turned-over trash can, dead Christmas lights dangling off the roofs of how many still houses?

Being alone didn't cut it anymore. It was odd how it happened. It happened the way Hemingway described going bankrupt—gradually, then suddenly. It seemed to happen this way, sooner or later, to everyone she knew.

Although Autry's house was cold, there would be voices. Voices meant distraction, and in this way, she could avoid direct contact with reality. But, oh, of course she didn't believe in the Project.

She wanted to drift while Ran drove, but when she closed her eyes, he began to talk. "Who's the dude?" he asked.

She searched the reaches of her side-view mirror to make sure Michael wasn't following them. He wasn't. She was relieved, then vaguely disappointed. She slouched back in her seat, resting her head on the play from the seatbelt. "A friend."

"Friend with benefits?"

She looked out the window.

"That's like where I'm at now," he went on. "Diamond took me out for Halloween last weekend. We went to the bars because she wanted to sing karaoke."

"What did you dress up as?"

"Oh, I didn't put on a costume. I can't pretend to be anything but myself. It's just who I am."

"Oh."

"I mean, it's the way I'm wired, I just have to be me."

"What did Diamond go as?"

"A sexy witch."

She sighed. "I like Halloween. I like pretending not to be me. What's not to like?"

"Halloween is every woman's favorite holiday," Ran said.

Oh, god, she thought. She glanced at him, then moved her eyes back to the highway, to its blinking theater of cars.

"It's true," he said. He looked at her.

She looked out the window again.

"Isn't it?" he went on.

"No."

"Well, okay—maybe not their *favorite* favorite holiday. They like Valentine's Day, too. Last year, Kayleigh, my girl-friend, got mad because I forgot to get her something. I guess she wanted chocolate, like a Whitman's Sampler. Something like that. So . . ." He waited for her to respond. "What do you think?"

"I don't know. I'm really tired, Ran."

He switched hands on the wheel. "Are you sad today, lady?"

"No, why?"

"What else did you do besides hang out with mystery dude?"

"Donated plasma."

"You voted, right?"

"Oh. Yeah. It's such an important election and all . . ." She trailed off. "What did you do today?"

"Co-op. And took boxes of my lip balm and pottery to the Himalayan—they're selling it for real now, which is pretty cool. They have orders for the lip balm in Saint Louis and Tulsa now."

"Wow, really?" She was genuinely impressed. "What's it called?"

"Ozark Mountain All-Natural Lip Butter."

"That's cool, Ran."

"I don't know about"—he took his hand off the wheel to slick his hair back—"cool."

"I'm serious. There's a lot of people out there trying to do something—something like that." Autry's face obliterated her headspace. How could she have actually slept with him? "But you're actually doing it."

"I fixed Destiny's transmitter. Shot some pool. I beat the shit out of some college bros. They were *bros*, man—Sigma Douchebag Sigma. Too bad we weren't putting money on the table."

She looked behind her. Canvas bags of groceries were in the seats. In front of her, the sky purpled over the mountains, and soon they were passing the familiar ditches of weeds and skeletal trees, the torn-down barns, the pond that had turned into a sheet of leaves. She unbuckled her seatbelt and stretched across the seat. She put her head in his lap and closed her eyes. "You don't mind, do you?"

"What?" She felt his whole body stiffen.

"I'm just going to close my eyes for a second."

"Okay." After a while he touched her hair, then brought his hand back to the wheel.

She woke up with the last turn before their driveway. She rubbed her eyes and sat up as they made their way up the gravel. A maroon van was parked in the grass, beside the shed.

"Ya'll got company?" Ran said. While he steered into his usual spot, she sat there dumbly, looking at Jim's maroon van.

She considered the familiar dents, the roof. She could not, as the saying goes, believe her eyes. It was like checking her bank statement on the computer screen at BioLife—the number was so low that she had trouble seeing it clearly.

It had been almost a year—ten months—since she'd seen him, and now he was here. Now he was *here?*

"I'll help you take this stuff in," Ran said. "Then I've got to head out, lady."

"Wait, no, no. No."

"What do you mean?"

"No. You can't leave yet. Don't leave."

"I've got work to do, but . . . I might, could stay for a minute. Why is your voice all high and weird?"

Jim was standing at the edge of the back deck, wearing a blue trucker hat she'd never seen and blue jeans rolled to his ankles. He exhaled a white thread of cigarette smoke as he listened to Autry talk. Rachel stood with them, wrapped in a quilt she clutched with both hands at her heart.

Chloe sat in one of the chairs that bounced, drowning in an oversize black coat with a strip of fur glued around the hood. Two mugs sat on the table, and she sipped from one of them.

"Holy shit, Chloe's out of bed," Ran said. "I haven't seen her up and walking around in a *while*. She's small. She looks like an ant."

Ellie stepped out of the truck and shut the door. "Ran," she said, as they lifted the groceries from the backseat, "you can't leave."

"Who is that guy?"

"My, whatever, my ex-boyfriend."

"Holy shit. Want me to kick his ass?"

"Just come with me. Please. I love you, please don't leave."

"What?"

"What?"

"What did you say?"

"I love you? Don't leave."

"Follow me," he said. She followed him to the back deck, staring at the heels of his shoes.

Chloe looked up from her hood and smiled, but her eyes were flat and sick.

"Nice to see you up and about," Ran told her, and gave her a high-five.

"Hey there, Ellie," Jim said. "How are you? How are you doing?" He said this with such wholesomeness and good nature it seemed almost sinister.

"This is a surprise," Ellie said. "Hey—so this is Ran."

"Howdy," Jim said.

"Okay," Ran said.

"Gorgeous spot y'all've got yourselves here," Jim said.

"Yeah. It is pretty. Ran grew up here," Ellie told Jim. "He's an amazing farmer, and he makes this lip balm from nothing—from scratch—and he's selling it everywhere. He's extremely talented."

"Yeah?" Jim said, looking at Ran.

Ran cleared his throat awkwardly and carried the groceries inside.

Rachel said, "Hey, Ellie—" but Ellie wasn't paying attention to anything except Jim, and the fact that he was standing there, in front of her face.

"He also makes pottery," she went on.

Chloe sipped from her mug.

"I don't know what we would do without him, I honestly don't," Ellie said. She glanced at Autry. She would pay for this tomorrow. And the next day. He would sulk and pout, and go on walks by himself, and Rachel would be guilty by association.

Jim looked at the smudged line of the mountains. Then he looked back at her, and they stared at each other again. There was a moment of hesitation before she stepped toward him, still with one bag of groceries in her arm, and hugged him.

He held her lightly. They let go.

He picked up the other mug on the table and stared into it.

"Well, I guess we have to get this stuff in," Ellie said, but she set the bag down. Ran would get it.

"Do you want to come in?" she said. "I mean—do you want to hang out? What are you drinking?"

"Hot tea," he said. "Mighty good, too."

Ran came back outside, and Rachel was tugging Ellie's arm now. "Come inside, come on—let me help you with this stuff," Rachel said, and picked up the canvas totes Ellie had set down.

Ellie started to follow Rachel, then whirled around. "Bye!" She threw her arms around Ran's neck.

"Oh," Ran said. "Okay. Love you. Later everyone."

"Later," Autry muttered.

Ran turned around. "Call me," he said to Ellie. "If you need—you know, anything."

Rachel took her into the bedroom—her and Autry's bedroom—and closed the door. "I am *so* sorry," Rachel said.

"What do you mean?"

"Well—I guess Chloe invited him."

"Chloe?"

"She didn't tell us, of course. I mean, I didn't think he was coming." Rachel readjusted the quilt around her shoulders— Ellie's quilt from self-storage. Rachel's cheeks were flushed with the cold, and her red hair was frizzed and coppery in this light, the color of wire.

Ellie stared at her for answers.

"How do they even fucking know each other?" Ellie finally said.

"I think Jim and Chloe are together," Rachel went on. "Like, together-together. They're weird around each other, polite and secretive. He was up in her room for about an hour as soon as he got here," Rachel said softly, and the pity in her voice—Ellie couldn't stand it. "They finally came down . . ."

She felt as if someone had reached into her chest bone and pressed.

"And I had to listen to Jim go on and on—asking, why is Chloe so skinny? How did she get this sick?" Rachel went on. "He goes, 'All she talks about is health, but everyone looks like they're dying.' Then *she* came down and said that she was fine, she really was—and, I don't know, they're, *together*."

"Stop. Stop. Stop—stop." Was she shrieking? "I already know this. So stop." She bit her nails, trying to piece it together. Phoenix's boots under Chloe's bed. A Crush Heat Burn show. Chloe's secret nightly phone calls she didn't think anyone knew about. Yeah, she knew. The instinct was to say, but why Chloe? She was *bald*, for crying out loud.

"I got it, I know," Ellie said to Rachel. "And I'm not concerned about it. It's the least of my concerns, actually."

"Okay," Rachel said, nodding. She touched Ellie's arm.

"I mean, what I'm concerned about," Ellie said, steadying her voice, "are the real problems of the world—like population growth."

Rachel nodded. "Yes."

"We're going to keep destroying the earth," Ellie went on, knowing she could escape like this forever, if she wanted to, with Rachel. Rachel wouldn't stop her. "As long as people keep trying to get people pregnant, we have no chance. Do you understand what I'm saying?"

"Of course. Of course, I do. Who could understand better. Go on . . ."

In the morning, Ellie lay in bed, staring at the ceiling. She coughed a little. She listened to her cold slide between her ears.

She replayed yesterday backward and forward.

She found Jim's morality and pretend-wholesomeness revolting. It was as if his image was wholesome enough, he couldn't be held accountable for anything. Anyone this fucking folksy must be blameless.

Had he *always* been like that? Yes, she realized. And she had actually *liked* it. Her recklessness in the weeks after they broke up was, in fact, probably a counterreaction.

It struck her that *health* was a synonym for *wholesomeness*.

The door creaked open. Rachel. "Breakfast? Obama was elected last night. Isn't that amazing?"

"Oh, wow. Thank god. Can you imagine if—"

"No."

"Is everybody down there?"

"I don't know where Autry is. Obama, Ellie."

"Sorry. I know. I know, holy shit, Obama."

"He's on a walk, presumably." She sat down on the edge of the bed. Ellie lifted the blankets for her, and they snuggled.

"What did he say about Jim being here and everything?" Ellie asked.

"Oh, he's acting like Jim's here to see *him*. Like he knew he was coming all along. Like it was part of his plan. Obama!"

"I know, it's amazing. I can't believe Barack Obama is our president."

"I know. He's so hot."

Jim and Chloe stood at the stove frying onions in the skillet, really the only thing to eat at the moment, each holding a spatula. He was making Chloe laugh with a story about a girl who worked at Dillard's. Ellie poured herself a cup of black coffee. Its steam rose into the cool air of the kitchen. Sunlight pushed against the glass doors.

She took her coffee into the great room by the fire, and knelt beside it. Heat rose through her body, into her cheeks.

Chloe and Jim. Their easy talk and laughter stung her.

She made a decision: She would be utterly polite. She would wage a war of kindness. She would pretend there was nothing surprising about Chloe and Jim being together, it was the most natural thing in the world, and she was very happy for them.

She went to the kitchen and put on boots. She stuffed

her jeans into them and walked outside. She dragged the red wagon through the shadows of tree limbs, to the woodpile at the top of the driveway, between the cars. She threw a few logs onto the wagon, then wiped her nose with her coat sleeve.

Rachel was hitting tennis balls against the side of the house. *Thwock. Thwock. Thwock.*

"Hey," Ellie called out.

Rachel turned and squinted, sweating a little, racquet under her arm.

Ellie walked over to her. "Where's that book about the woman living off all the shit in her house?"

"*Not Buying It*? I don't know. Somewhere."

Ellie went inside and looked for it.

When Autry got back from his walk a half-hour later, he took off his shirt and threw it on the floor of the great room. Jim came down with his banjo. They started playing old-time music and jug band tunes.

Chloe took a very long shower, then stood next to the record player. When they took a break, Ellie said, "That was really good," and clapped a little. She looked at Jim. She wanted to provoke him, surprise him. "You know, you're really quite talented."

He looked at her. "What?"

He'd heard what she'd said, but she repeated it anyway. Then: "I don't know. Never mind."

"Oh. Thank you?" he said. He said this in his regular voice.

Listening, she began to worry about watching ASMR—worried that she wouldn't be able to relax with Jim and Chloe sitting there. She wouldn't be able to let go, like trying to escape in a novel with someone reading over your shoulder.

Eventually, she went to the kitchen. When nobody was looking, she took the phone off the hook, and put it in the pocket of her sweatshirt. She walked toward the stairs.

"Where are you going?" Autry said, startling her. He had just come from the bathroom.

"Upstairs," she said. "To get dressed."

"Dressed? What do you mean, you're fucking dressed right now."

"To—put more clothes on. I'm cold."

"I'm doing the best I can to bring the wood in and keep the fire going." He rubbed his fingers through his hair in a violent stroke.

"Okay," she said, and continued up the stairs. She opened the cover of *Not Buying It* and called Ran. He answered the phone as though he had been waiting for it to ring.

He picked her up the next morning, with the radio playing louder than usual, the bass turned on, so her seat vibrated when she clicked the belt over her lap. He'd shaved off the beginnings of his beard, and his hair looked slicked back with products. He told her he was going to play pool today for money. She wondered if he'd recently watched *The Hustler* or something.

The day was gray and cool, with a layer of fog folded over the mountain. "Thanks for coming," she said.

"Look, is somebody in that house bothering you? Autry? The ex-boyfriend? Because, I swear to god I'll . . . I'll . . . fucking . . ."

"Let's get out of here," she said, saving him from having to finish the sentence.

"What did you tell everyone?"

"The truth." It *was*, in a way, sort of truthful. "That I needed to get away for a day and night. I only told Rachel. I don't give a fuck what Autry thinks. Don't repeat that. Rachel understands, that's all I care about."

"You and Rachel are tight."

"Even when we're loose, we're tight."

Rain began to tap the hood of the truck. The windshield became dotted with its soft bites. He turned on the wipers, and she asked what he'd been up to.

"Just helping my beloved little old people." He always made his parents seem elderly, but they were only in their forties.

Wind bent all the trees they passed. The XM radio was tuned to Ran's favorite station, the one that played Top Country: Today's Hits. An overproduced father-son song was playing that went:

Knowing that he couldn't have the toy
Till his nuggets were gone
A green traffic light turned straight to red
I hit my brakes and mumbled under my breath
His fries went a-flying and his orange drink covered his lap

"So they don't have yellow lights where they live," Ellie said.

"Huh?"

"Can we listen to something else?"

"Why—you don't like country? I thought you liked country."

"I like *country*."

"That's what I just said." He shook his head. "You're a weird chick."

Finally, they were in the front loop of the hotel. He said, "You good?"

She nodded.

"You sure you don't want some company? Sure you don't want me to go in with you?"

"Yeah, I just need some time alone. By myself. I need some self storage."

"Self what?"

"I'll be fine."

"Well, see you in the morning, right? Right here?"

She nodded, opened the door, and stepped outside. A strong gust of wind whipped her hair back. Her cardigan flagged behind her at her back. "Good luck at pool," she said.

"Don't blow away."

She walked through the rotating hotel doors, into the front lobby with its white marble floor. Fake ivy twisted around twin fountains by the curved stairwell. Behind the front desk, a gray-suited woman wearing a nameplate gave Ellie her keycard.

The elevator lifted her to the seventh floor. She was all alone. She felt the silence of the hallway beat inside her head. She found the room and opened the heavy door.

She stood in the middle of the room, letting her purse fall off her shoulder. She collapsed luxuriously onto the huge bed and stared at the panels on the ceiling. It had been over five months since she'd had sex. She wondered: What if everything had changed? What if all the rules were different now? What if all the masturbation in the past few months had changed some kind of makeup inside her?

She turned up the heat and took a long bath that filled the room with steam. Then her eye caught the Nanette Lepore dress hanging on the back of the door in a long plastic bag. It was green knit with long sleeves that flared slightly at the wrists. She touched the fabric, thinking how lucky she was that somebody really knew her.

Michael let himself in a little after five. He threw his keys on the floor, by the door—his old joke from her tiny apartment.

She stood in front of him.

He put his hands in his pockets. "Turn around," he said.

She turned around.

"But we're still going to go out to dinner though and everything," Ellie said, reaching for her drink on the nightstand. "Right?"

"Nah," he said. "Nah. I thought we'd just lay here for the rest of the night."

She looked at him. "Oh."

"I'm kidding." He squeezed her hip. "Tell me a haiku. Tell me a very sexy one."

She thought for a moment.

"I'm waiting," he said.

"A prostitute's shack / at the edge of town / in the autumn wind."

"A prostitute's shack?"

"Visiting the graves / the old dog / leads the way."

"These aren't sexy . . ."

"Bats flitting here and there; / the woman across the street / glances this way."

"You're doing this on purpose." He laughed and she got on top of him, her legs bent on either side of him.

She leaned over and kissed him. He touched the middle of her chest, where her heart was.

"You're the worst," he said.

The shadows from the lamplight made his face dark and ethereal as he put his hands behind his head like a pillow. "Don't move," he said. "Let me look at you." Wind sang against the side of the hotel; it cried through the four corners of the huge window. "Where are the stuffed dogs?" he said. "You didn't get rid of them, did you?"

"Of course not. They're in my bag."

"An overnight bag, look at you."

She smiled and finished her drink. "Let's go," she said. She stood up and brushed her hair.

She buttoned Michael's shirt for him. The clock on the nightstand read eight thirty in bright red numbers. At the next eight thirty, Ran would be here, circling into the front loop of the hotel. "Wait," she said.

She wanted to make the time stop. Michael-feelings bounced in the walls of her brain like shapes on a screensaver. She wanted to tell him something, but the sentences were in these big blobby forms, swimming in her head.

Here, standing at the hotel window at *this* eight thirty, it seemed easy to believe in happiness. But she had to consider the next eight thirty—when she would be alone again, with a hangover, returning to the voices of the house.

"What is it?" he said.

"Nothing," she replied, and leaned against his chest. He stroked her hair. They stood there, as if against the wind.

VII

THREE IN THE AFTERNOON

RACHEL

APRIL 2009

Rachel came awake facing the window, and the grass and sky that colored it every single solitary morning. Through it, a horse stood at the fence with its long head dipped into some weeds. Insects walked on the other side of the pane, among dead insects. She shut her eyes and dug back to sleep.

But Autry dropped his book about making your own dairy products on the floor, and the bed squeaked as he turned on his side and pressed his knees against the backs of her knees. He wrapped both arms around her.

"Did you dream about me?" he whispered.

She felt held like a stuffed animal. His breath was so hot and familiar on her neck, as though she were somehow incestuously breathing on herself. She made a noise that could have meant anything—yes, no, what was the question?

"I thought so," he said. "I could tell because you were smiling."

Oh, god, she was tired of him.

Her face—it couldn't have been smiling. She kept her back to him, cheek pressed to the pillow. He began to trace circles between her shoulders blades, down the track of her spine.

Okay, these circles—they began to work.

This was what remained of their relationship. She woke up with this heartbeat between her legs every morning, this need, what could she say? Otherwise, she was so sick of him it bordered on mania.

She could put it this way: He was a body now. He got the job done. That was mean, probably. But what if this were *it*? Sometimes you heard about those marriages where the wives faked it. She didn't think she could live like that.

She considered her other lovers. There weren't many, because she was the relationship kind—two years here, three years there, always living together. She had heard that great sex was rare—but how rare? Just how rare, she kept wondering. She would ask Ellie. Ellie would know. Ellie should *definitely* know.

A plane was in the window now, dragging its long white mark through the sky. Rachel wanted to be on it. Autry drew circles lower and lower on her back, on her sides, so that she felt a sensation close to being tickled, except infinitely better.

She imagined the black carry-ons being lifted overhead, the spiral loops of a beige phone cord stretched between pilot and attendant. A drink cart was rolling down the aisle, and through the window, she was gliding over the blue kidneys and guitars that were swimming pools.

She wanted to be on that plane. She wanted engines, she wanted dryers, she wanted space heaters. She wanted chicken nuggets that weren't totally chicken, and hot baths with scented bubbles and Coke. She wanted her toes painted in a salon with Vietnamese women passing secrets over her ankles. She wanted to stand in front of a wall full of brightly colored nail polish, with names like MIAMI BEET and THERE'S NO PLACE LIKE CHROME. She wanted a sign with WALK-INS WELCOME blinking in neon.

Now he was kissing her shoulder, now her collarbone. She kept her eyes closed and positioned her head in a way that made it impossible for him to kiss her mouth. Finally his tongue hardened between her legs, and let's face it, there was nothing like Autry doing this—nothing. He didn't stop until her legs shook around his shoulders and involuntary laughter escaped her. Then came the despair that followed the ecstasy, after he turned her over to finish on her back.

He reached for the towel on the floor to clean her spine, her sides. He fell back into bed and groaned, and she thought she wanted, at that moment, to die.

They lay there, still as knives.

"One day your parents are going to come by," she said. "We haven't *done* anything."

"They wouldn't just show up, like unannounced."

"We haven't done anything," she yawned.

"Here we go again. Anyway, how can you say that?" He patted her leg. "We just got one thing done."

She couldn't stand this man.

"I'm not worried about it," Autry continued. "Who cares if they do come? I'll just explain about the Project. They'll like it—it's noble."

"Mm."

"What?"

"I didn't say anything."

"I'm cutting the path we have to take before I can write about it—researching and learning through our experiences. I mean, anyway, my parents love me. You act like it's the KGB that's coming."

She heard Chloe upstairs, turning in her bed, making sounds of pain. "*Annnd* she's awake," Rachel sighed.

"Again," he said. "What do you want me to do about it? Jim's back. He came back last night. She always gets better when he comes back. She'll heal . . . She will. She just needs time. We need to give her time."

"I think she might be, like—actually sick."

"We can't see our reflection in running water. It's only in still water that we can see."

Oh, good god, she hated this man.

Jim had come and gone and come and gone ever since

Election Day. He went to music festivals, and down to Fay-etteville. This time, he'd been playing in Kansas City and Saint Louis for two weeks, opening for Muddy Graves.

Chloe rallied a little each time he came back, but then he'd go away again to play music. Was he just using her for a place to stay? Rachel wondered this often.

Rachel said, "I honestly think we should call Ran and—"

"That's enough," he said. He swung his legs over the edge of the bed.

Part of her believed that if she annoyed him enough, then he would have to do something about her. Then something would have to happen.

"I'm getting up now," he said.

"Wait."

"No—why are you doing this? Why is every morning a fucking inquisition? Ran has no appreciation for the Project, no appreciation for our way of life, he's ignorant, he doesn't know shit." He picked up his khakis and angrily shook out the legs to step into.

Rachel wondered how she could have once thought that this man—this man standing here in the middle of the bed-room—was cool. But she had. A previous Rachel, one of her former selves, had actually *loved* him. It seemed ridiculous, but she had.

She had so many former selves now; she worried she would unravel and divide into all the copies she'd made of herself.

He left the room without a shirt, a notebook under an arm and his pen behind one ear. For what? The notebook was empty.

She stretched into the middle of the bed, where a cool crest down the center of the mattress separated the two sides. She daydreamed about sleeping on this high, cool crest. Eventually, she forced herself out of bed.

The weather was mild again, so living off-grid was tolerable. This had been the SouthWestern Electric Power Company's decision—not theirs. They hadn't paid a bill in months and now the power had been cut off. But in the book—this week titled *Reflections on Living in Health*—it would be their decision to live without electricity. In the book version of their lives, the decision comes after many nights of philosophical argument and reasoning. They were choosing to live this way, in the book.

Autry's pseudo philosophical deep talk made her nauseous now. He said it helped him to talk about it—*then* he would write it all down.

Living off-grid wasn't bad though, Rachel told herself. It wasn't bad. It was *not* bad, and it was still her decision. She was choosing to be here, she told herself.

Besides, they still had water, it just wasn't hot. Who needed hot water? A family of four wasted over ten thousand gallons of water a year waiting for hot water to reach their showers and sinks.

She walked into the kitchen and tied the apron across her bony waist one more time. Jim was sitting at the table on the back deck, drinking sun tea, staring into the mountain and its morning shadows.

Flies circled the ceiling, and sugar ants stayed hectic among the dirty dishes.

She picked up a pitcher of juice on the counter and drank from the lip. The fruit had disintegrated and smeared against the sides of the pitcher. Once upon a time, this had grossed her out. Now, she didn't care. The juice was warm and she didn't care.

She would drink anything, eat anything lying around. She wiped her mouth with the back of her hand. She reached into the glass jar and scooped out a handful of stale granola—which was mostly oat. She went outside with her mouth full, in her flannel shirt and underwear, her legs white with winter. The freckles around her knees and wrists had paled, but the sunspot under her eye hadn't disappeared all season.

"Hey," she said to Jim. "Welcome back. How was your tour?"

Jim gave her a head nod. "Oh, the tour was amazing. These festivals are just so good for us—I met some great folks who really just dug the music."

The air was fragrant with the beginnings of spring, foreign on her tongue when she breathed. Random bursts of color—the violets, the buttercups, the anemone—tried to cheer the yard. The plum trees were in bloom.

She sat down. A sweet, warm breeze brushed through her hair.

"So anyway," Jim said.

She braced herself.

"I really appreciate all the time I've had here," he said. "I've been able to write a whole 'nother album of songs. Ya'll are so great, and you're such a good person—and you're just real generous to have put me up. But I think, I think it's time—I gotta go, you know? Agnes called, she has some shows lined up for me."

"But I'm sure Chloe's really happy to see you," Rachel said. "Don't you want to spend time here? I really think she's doing much better. I mean, we're doing the best we can—we're not doctors."

"No, you're not. That's another reason we're going to head back."

"You're leaving together?"

"Yeah, she probably needs to see someone."

"She doesn't have health insurance."

"Who has fucking health insurance?"

"Autry does. His parents pay for it. Where are you going to go?"

"She's got some money saved from Viceory—I made a little from tips on the tour. I signed us up a lease, a studio apartment. It's right above Natalie's, so it's perfect for shows and stuff."

"So you're going to like, stay in Fayetteville?"

"Well, I'm still going to have to travel—I'm a musician, I'm always going to have to travel. I'm just saying I need to take her back. This shower stuff is fucking nuts, anyway. Look, sometimes I wake up in the middle of the night, and I find her standing in the shower, in her clothes. Not showering, I mean. She's just standing there, without the water on, looking at the showerhead."

"It's all just in her mind."

"*Yep*. That's the trouble."

"Sometimes we can only see our reflection in still water . . ." Rachel started, and trailed off. She didn't have the heart.

"What?"

"Nothing."

"I need to step up," Jim went on. "She needs me, you know?" He was speaking with real feeling. She had never heard him speak like this—with passion. Even when he talked about music, it was with that detached country persona.

"She likes it here."

"That's the hell of it—just this morning, she told me that she really wanted to keep living in health here. It's like she's brainwashed." He shook his head. "In *health*. Right? Like the world's healthiest diet is going to kill you."

Rachel opened a window in the great room. Late-morning sun spilled through it and hit a lampshade, so it looked turned on. Wind blew through the screen, and with it, dust lifted from under the furniture and floated in the air. His grandmother's cushions stared back at her from their positions on the sofa. Maybe she would clean today, she thought doubtfully.

At first, Rachel, too, had been surprised that Jim and Chloe were together. She pictured seldom sex, seldom orgasms. But it made sense now: Jim felt heroic taking care of her, and Chloe wasn't going to break his heart. They didn't have to play the who-cares-less game. And probably, her being sick and bald made him feel more interesting.

Besides, he needed somewhere to live.

Ellie didn't seem to mind their relationship anymore. She even seemed happy these days, but Rachel couldn't figure out why.

So, it would be the three of them again, Rachel thought. Her boyfriend and her best friend—like the early days. They would be fine.

Autry came behind her, startling her. She actually almost flinched. He fitted his hands around her waist. "Ray," he said, whispering on her neck, making goose bumps run down the side of her body. "I'm sorry about earlier, okay. Everything's going to be all right. You have to trust me." They heard the clang of drawers upstairs in Chloe's room, shoes. "What's with all that?" he said.

"I don't know," Rachel shrugged. *She* wasn't going to tell him.

"I'm going to smoke a bowl and read," he said.

"Okay."

Soon, it would be June. She could make it until June.

It's not like she had other plans, anything waiting in the real world—which seemed completely daunting. Money. Clothes. A job. A car. An apartment. Keys. Taxes. Facebook. Credit cards. Alarms and notifications. She wondered if she could even do these things, when it was time. She wondered if it wouldn't be so bad, after all, to just stay here.

She tied on her running shoes, then stepped outside again.

She hit tennis balls against the side of the house. The balls were flat, but she preferred them this way, so she could swing as hard as she wanted, which felt good. The *beat-beat* sound against the side of the house was soothing like ASMR. She hit all morning.

When Ellie finally reentered the world from her shell of bedsheets and stuffed animals, she was barefoot in thin white shorts and a faded T-shirt with razorback heads all over it. She sat Indian-style in the gravel and played with the braid in her hair while she watched Rachel hit.

When she was through, Rachel sat next to her. She took her shoes off in the sun, stretched her legs out in front of her, and sighed. "They're leaving tonight, you know."

Ellie nodded. "They're up there packing."

"What are they taking? I mean . . . it's all communal at this point. They have to leave her car here . . . at least."

"Oh. Otherwise—"

"Exactly. Think about being stuck here."

"Oh well. We can make it until June." Ellie stood up and did a cartwheel in the gravel.

Why was she happy? Rachel couldn't figure it out.

Ellie dusted off her hands. "Let's walk."

They walked. They walked slow and wobbly because the driveway's gravel dug into their feet, like old ladies walking. It rained yesterday and the gravel rocks were always sharper on the bottom of their feet after it rained.

"What time do you think it is?" Ellie said.

"Maybe three?" The sun was obscured behind a white sky, as if they were walking against a backdrop. Without clocks and electricity, time was erased, and somehow it always seemed like three. Three P.M. or three A.M. It was a reasonable guess.

Rachel truly wasn't sure if Autry would be disappointed or glad that Jim and Chloe were leaving. He did hate to be abandoned. He had even asked her to marry him. On Christmas Day, he'd planted himself down on one knee in the middle of the great room. A tree they'd dragged inside and strung with popcorn and ornaments of trash with paper clips for hooks stood stupidly in the corner.

"Not until *everyone* can get married," was her response. She figured a lot of people used this excuse. By the time gay marriage was actually legal, hopefully the relationship would be over. She would be on a plane by then.

Rachel wasn't ready to tell Ellie about wanting to break up with Autry, and Ellie didn't ask. It was a respect thing. When she was ready, Rachel could say "*Again . . .*" in Autry's voice. Then they could make fun of him, and clear the air.

It worked both ways. Ellie never explained about the time she stayed overnight in Fayetteville, for example. Ran brought her back home in a green dress, her knees bruised, mascara under her eyes—unhealth written all over her face.

Without electricity, ASMR was tricky—they couldn't watch the videos. So they escaped in other ways. Instead of immersing themselves in hours of soft hair-brushing, for example, the clink of nails on a wooden desk, fake doctor's visits and brain exams, consultations for trips to unknown planets, they got lost in their own heads. They traded turns talking in stream-of-conscious monologues. After a while, they weren't even listening to each other, it was more about just filling the air with the comfortable lilts and turns of story.

They walked to the creek like this, while small birds chatted in the tree limbs above them. Every time they walked to the creek, Rachel thought about how both animals and humans went to the water to die.

A teenage memory returned to her: an oceanfront house with a wraparound deck, and a line of empty rocking chairs facing the ocean. Next door, a man with a blanket over his legs, even though it was ninety-five in the shade, sat facing the horizon of sea and sky all day.

Rachel knew, without exactly knowing, that he was dying. His eyes would always be closed, chin lifted to the salty waves as the ice cream truck circuited the neighborhood with its chimes. The family was from Ohio; he'd asked them to take him to the ocean.

This was back when she was just an eleventh grader, back when her family was still her family, before her father died, before her mother had remarried and started another family, then divorced and remarried again—before anything important had ever happened to her.

Rachel had been talking for some time now about the man at the beach, when Ellie knelt by the creek and splashed water on her face. Its coolness took her breath away. Rachel put a toe in, and watched the dust and dirt uncurl over a rock, into the tiny current.

· · ·

Sun burned through a brief clearing in the sky, and then there was the noise of a far-off engine. It was unmistakable, the sound of wheels on gravel, on the road that led to their driveway. A car. Their soothing talk fell off a cliff.

Rachel made a visor with her hand to shade her eyes. She listened.

They looked at each other.

"Autry's parents," Rachel said.

"Wait." Ellie stared in concentration.

"What should we do?"

Ellie closed her eyes. "I'll go see." She opened them. "I think it's nobody. You're paranoid."

"Who's nobody?"

"I'll be right back." She started walking toward the road, stepping over a fallen tree limb, then began to run.

Rachel checked the urge to follow her. She felt in her bones that it was Autry's parents. *So what if it was?* she wondered, but it didn't help her paranoia.

She would not move from this spot until Ellie came back. She combed the grass around her ankles, searching for four-leaf clovers. She found one, stared at it in complete wonder, then ripped it up. She lay back with an arm over her eyes.

She sat up. Why hadn't Ellie come back? Had five minutes passed, or twenty-five? A half hour? She beat a path through the trees, toward the road.

At the bottom of the hill was a black car stalled between some bushes. She swallowed. The police, in an unmarked car. They were here to arrest her. But it wasn't the police.

Ellie was in the passenger seat, turned so that the back of her head obscured the other person's.

Rachel stood beside the passenger door. "Um."

They turned and looked at her.

Ellie laughed nervously. "I didn't know he was coming here," she explained, looking to the man beside her for help. She put her fingers to her mouth.

"Michael," he said, extending his hand. "Lindsey. Pleased to meet you." He was good-looking, in a boring way, with a clean-shaven face and straight, artificially white teeth.

"I know who you are," Rachel said. "You're the Walmart guy, right?"

He put his hands up. "You got me."

Weeks ago, Ellie mentioned his name, her former boss, in passing—during an ASMR-like monologue. Rachel didn't know they were actually still *friends*.

She took his hand, which looked and felt brilliantly clean, and shook it. He smiled at her. "And you are?"

"What do you even *do* at Walmart?"

"Oh, leave him alone, Ray, be nice," Ellie started to tell her. "He's okay."

"Cashier," Michael said. "I stock shelves."

This made Ellie laugh.

"Seriously," Rachel said. "I'd like to know *exactly* what your business is there. Officially. But in your own words."

"You must be Rachel," he said.

She didn't reply.

"Rachel—come on, get in. He's not that bad," Ellie said, leaning against Michael's shoulder. A bottle of Rumple

Minze sat between them against the gear shift. "We've already taken some shots, so."

"How about a drink," Michael told Rachel. "You must need one, right?"

"Come on, just one," Ellie pleaded. "If you drink with me right now, I promise to smoke more weed with you."

"You always say that, but you never do."

"Please."

Michael poured a whisper of Rumple Minze into a little plastic cup, as if from a hotel, then handed it to her. "Just a little one," he said.

The empty gravel road rolled out in front of them like a long gray carpet. "I'm not going to waste a plastic cup," Rachel said. She wasn't going to leave Ellie here. She got in the backseat. Autry would be furious—crushed. The thought made her feel lighter.

"Drink out of the bottle," Michael said.

It had been a year since Rachel had drunk anything, and she'd never liked the way alcohol tasted. It nauseated her most of the time. Through college, at Fayetteville bars and at parties in tiny, carpeted apartments, she drank Sprite over crushed ice. Meanwhile, Ellie would drink enough whiskey or gin not to be herself anymore.

"How did you know how to get here?" Rachel asked.

Ellie handed her the bottle. "Does it matter?"

She took a sip and it burned her throat. It tasted like mouthwash and rubbing alcohol. Her face twisted—she felt it—and she wiped her mouth.

"Take another," Ellie said. "It's good."

Rachel put it to her lips again, and Ellie pushed it back until Rachel swallowed, forcing it down.

For a fast instant she was about to throw up. But she swallowed it down.

Ellie and Michael began to talk.

The disgusting taste passed, passed gloriously, and something else took hold. She slouched against the leather seat, weightless and happy as air. She liked the way the leather sounded when she crossed her legs. A hole had opened in her brain, and her troubles curved and evaporated through it.

"We need music," Ellie said. Michael reached over and opened the glove compartment for her. She rifled through his caseless CDs with handwriting on the faces of the disks. "So Michael is actually like a sixty-year-old black man," Ellie said.

Rachel laughed, because it felt good to laugh.

"We've got Bill Withers here, James Brown, Motown, Bobby Womack . . ." Ellie said, going through the CDs.

"Oh, girls," Michael said smiling.

Rachel and Ellie laughed again. Every time they looked at each other, there was the feeling of an inside joke.

"I want us all to get drunk," Ellie was saying.

Rachel watched the two of them pass the bottle back and forth.

"I can't drink anymore," Rachel said. "But I guess I'll have one more. Then let's go, Ellie."

"Where have you got to go? I'm just curious," Michael asked.

Rachel couldn't stop looking at this new face. She thought she probably wanted to run away with him. People were on planes right now, all over the world, descending runways, with the pilot reciting local time and temperature. She thought of the new faces and bodies that would be on the plane, in her next life. She realized how much she had been wanting, *craving* this: intimacy with a new person.

Intimacy with a stranger, even.

It clicked like her seatbelt, like crossing her legs: People besides Autry would know what to do.

She and Ellie moved their heads to the beat. Ellie looked completely altered, and Rachel remembered how this happened—how her whole face transformed when she became drunk. They were listening to a song that went *I want to spread the news, that if it feels this good getting used, you just keep on using me, until you use me up.*

Michael looked at Ellie as she drank from the bottle, then turned around to look at Rachel.

Rachel kept her eyes on him.

Ellie leaned her head back, and brought her arms around Rachel's neck, her head upside down over the headrest. Ellie kissed her, and Rachel kissed her back. Her mouth felt small and tender and new, like a sweet wound. She felt Michael stroking her hair. She opened her eyes, and saw his other hand in Ellie's hair. She closed her eyes again, and let it happen.

A late afternoon sunset the color of burnt grass was in the windshield, when she finally got out of the car. Heat lightning flickered in the distance.

"I'll be right behind you," Ellie promised, as Rachel opened the door and spilled out, dizzy.

Walking back through the trees, and then the field, everything whirled around her in a dark gray braid. The rocks in the gravel driveway weren't sharp against her feet anymore. In fact—what feet? She barely felt them attached to her body.

The space by the shed where Jim had parked his van was empty. She staggered onto the back deck, where Autry sat in a chair. She stood still, afraid to walk any further, afraid of giving herself away.

"Where were you," he said. He didn't turn his head.

"Oh," she said. "There you are."

He touched his mustache. "Seriously, where the fuck did you go?"

"Just—away—we just took a walk. Ellie's behind me. I'm going to take a shower." She tried to steady her voice, but she knew the harder she tried not to appear drunk, the drunker she probably appeared. She reminded herself to be very careful—to make sense. "So—they're gone?"

"*What?*" he said.

She spoke louder. "Jim and Chloe are gone?"

"Yeah. So? I always knew they were going to leave. Where did you go on your walk?"

"Just—around, to the creek and stuff. So I'm going to take a shower."

"All day?" He was looking at her now, the rims of his eyes pink with weed. He walked over to her, so they stood directly in front of each other. "Are you drunk?"

"No."

He looked directly into her eyes, straight through her. For a second, she actually loved him again. Then it passed.

"Ellie," he concluded.

"No."

"Yes. Ellie."

"No."

"Don't cover for her, it makes you look stupid. She's pathetic without health. She's the picture of unhealth."

"No . . ."

"All you do is hold me back." He crossed his arms. "You're not what I thought you were."

"Well, like—it's going to storm tonight and our roof leaks."

"You're slurring," he said with disgust. "You're not making any sense. From now on I'm keeping tabs on both of you. No more wandering around. No more wandering off."

"You can't tell me what to do."

"Yes, I can. Who are you? This is my house."

The handles on the glass doors rattled with the wind. She was going to be sick.

"I'm going to be sick," she said.

"You should see yourself." He shook his head. "I mean, really."

She watched him go inside.

Heat lightning flickered in the sky. A slant of rain was blowing in from the west, like a sheer curtain. She put her hands on her knees. Even when she closed her eyes, she saw the heat lightning wink and wink at her.

VIII

REAL

ELLIE

JUNE 2009

So how many demerits are you going to get for this," Michael said over the white noise of air conditioning, over the sex beats of an R&B station. They were in a bubble, a speeding capsule of time, with its cool vents slanted toward their faces. The world blurred past her window in a fine veil of dust.

She put her lips to the bottle of Jameson and drank.

"You know I want to kill this guy, right?"

"Not as much as Ran does," Ellie replied.

A clipboard was nailed to the front door, with a pen attached to a string for the three of them to explain where they were going, what they were doing, and when they would be back.

It was blank.

This afternoon, Ellie ran down the hill, through the trees, to the safe black car with Michael inside it and the seats that smelled like money.

"Go faster," she said, and watched his foot steel down on the pedal.

She threw her head back and closed her eyes. She could scream. "I'm happy right now," she said.

"So easy to please these days," he said. "I don't know about this."

"So?"

"So you're not getting sweet on me, are you?"

She smiled. "No. So what if I was?"

They were flying. The cold artificial air felt glorious on her arms, like a cool brush. "Faster."

He went faster. She opened her eyes. Mailboxes ticked off pieces of time. She drank.

They parked on a bank, under some trees, beside a few pickup trucks and an old school bus with weeds growing inside.

The water was gleaming, perfect.

He killed the engine. She drank from the bottle one more

time and Michael lifted a cooler out of the backseat. She carried the towels.

They stood at the edge of the White River, where the water cuffed their ankles. The water felt cold, almost too cold to wade. They stood there. "Come on," she said, finally.

She held her breath as she waded in. The water crept to her waist. Michael followed her. She could feel his eyes on her back; she liked that. She liked having someone watching her. But it was more than that—it was having someone watch *over* her.

They came to a pale rock with a flat surface, and lay on their backs. They talked about nothing while the breeze stirred the fringe of their towels. They drank beers. She liked the beads of water on Michael's chest. She liked the wind. She finished a beer, and opened another, and she liked the sound the tab made on the rock.

"Slow down," he said.

She liked his voice.

"No," she said.

He pulled out some bread he bought already flavored with olive oil, plus grape tomatoes, mozzarella, and leaves of basil to pinch off with their fingers. She ate a little.

"What do you think?" he asked.

"What an original combination," Ellie said.

"There's more." He pulled out kebobs of chicken and peppers and cold miniature crab cakes with spicy aioli—leftovers from the annual office picnic at the Lindseys' house.

Ellie picked one up. "Remember the party last year," she asked, breaking a piece of chicken from the kebob.

How odd to think the party was already nearly a year ago. Not long afterward, she'd driven here, passing the stench of the chicken coop, swearing off meat for Rachel and Autry—sort of. Now she didn't care. She'd eat cold chicken off a stick.

"I remember being locked in the bathroom with you," he said.

"That was crazy."

"Marianne thinks I'm seeing you again."

"Why does she think that?"

"Well, probably because I *am*. Things are kind of messy right now, honestly."

"When can you come back out here?"

"It's all a little complicated right now, is what I'm saying."

"Will you bring Chik-fil-A next time? A number five, with a twelve-pack of nuggets and a Coke."

"I don't know. We need to be somewhat careful from here on out. Marianne is—she's suspicious. Crazy."

"Most women are crazy."

Michael nodded.

"But women are crazy because men are stupid, generally speaking."

"I don't know about that."

"No, it's true." She drank her beer while he looked across the bank.

"Who's that?" he asked

She followed his gaze. Ran.

Ran was standing on a rock across from them, waving his

hat. Ellie stood and waved back, and they called out to each other. She looked at Michael. "It's Ran," she explained.

Ran waded in, and swam toward them. He was shirtless, with a backpack and a fishing pole. Water dripped from his shorts when he heaved himself onto their rock. His running shoes squeaked. She hugged him. He held her and said, "Hey, stranger."

She smiled and introduced him to Michael.

"See that girl over there?" Ran said. Ellie shielded the sun from her eyes and looked across the water. A thin long-haired girl who looked nineteen was standing in the sun on a rock.

"That's my girlfriend."

"She looks too sweet to be a stripper," Ellie said.

"Nah. She's not a stripper. She's in school to be a nurse."

"What kind of nursing?" Ellie asked.

"I don't know, it's—something where she has to wear scrubs."

Ellie offered him a beer.

"Oh, no, it's early," he said. Then: "Only cause I got so wasted last night. How's everyone?"

"Chloe and Jim are gone. They went back."

"You're not still donating plasma, are you? Your nose is running."

She sniffled. "No. No more plasma. I have a, uh—friend—who's been helping me out now," she said, looking at Michael, who wouldn't meet her eyes.

"Do I need to come out there?" Ran said.

"I'm going to kill that guy," Michael said.

"He's Rachel's dude," Ran said. "So I thought . . . I didn't know if ya'll wanted me around anymore. Not looking for trouble, not worth it, know what I mean? I mean, no offense. I just . . . can't stop laughing at him though."

Ran's girlfriend yelled to him from across the bank. He waved to her. "I gotta go. Do you need anything, Ellie? I'm serious, 'cause I'll come out your way. I'll be out that way anyway, next week, or the week after, to see my parents. I'm renting a little house in Fayetteville now, for the two of us."

"I thought you hated Fayetteville."

"We're on the outskirts, see. It just makes sense to be closer, because she's in school. And for business stuff. I'm thinking of buying a little house. I still go out and help my beloved little old people pretty often. I could bring you some venison."

"I'm moving back to Fayetteville, too," Ellie announced.

"Really?"

She nodded.

"Where? When?"

"I'm not exactly sure yet." She looked at Michael.

He smiled uneasily and shrugged. He looked away.

"Who knows," she added.

After Ran went away, they drank. Then a cloud moved over the sun. Goose bumps appeared over her wet body, and they went back to the parking lot.

They drove out a little ways, until they were alone in the weeds, under the trees with their thick branches. They made love, *real actual love*, Ellie thought. It was intimate and real and nonviolent. She couldn't believe it—she almost cried.

"I better get back," Michael said, putting his shirt on. He touched her chin. "Let's go. You ready?"

"No."

"Come on. I have to go."

"Why?"

"I have to."

While he drove, she played with the CDs in the CD changer. She told him that his music was stupid, even though she secretly approved of it, and was holding his hand while she said it, tracing the lines in his palm. She turned on the radio to a station playing nineties music, which had circled back into popularity. They listened to a Beck song that went, *So, I'm a loser baby, so why don't you kill me.* She found a Styrofoam cup under her seat and poured Jameson into it.

"Why bother with a cup now?" Michael said.

"I like pouring."

"She likes pouring."

"I like putting my teeth into the Styrofoam."

"Why?"

"It feels good."

Soon, bite marks made a ring around the lip of her cup.

"I thought you liked pain," he said, touching her crotch, still wet with sex and the river.

She looked at him. She needed to tell him that she was ready to be with him for real—it wasn't a joke anymore. They *weren't* just friends.

And she wanted him to tell her how he would blow up his life for her, like he did that day in his office, while she was sitting in his lap, when she knew that he loved her for certain. Was it crazy? Was this real? She didn't know, but it's what she wanted right now.

"How's your friend?"

"Rachel?"

"Are there others?"

"The same. Nothing to report."

"Nothing?"

"Why do you like to think that we have some kind of erotic relationship, just because of what happened last time?"

"I'm kidding."

"Faster." She closed her eyes.

He went faster.

He said, "Why is she with Autry, though? I don't get that one."

"She's not, really, anymore. What—are you fucking *interested*?"

"No, honey. Why you two don't leave?"

"We will. Soon."

"What are you waiting for?"

"I don't know. Something to happen, I guess."

"Like what?"

"I don't know." She felt under her seat, because her sunglasses had slipped away on the ride up. First she retrieved a plastic Walmart bag with plastic Walmart bags inside it.

"What are you looking for?" he asked.

"My sunglasses." She found them. She found all sorts of items down there: a ballpoint pen, old sections of the *Northwest Arkansas Democrat Gazette*, and then a baby monitor, brand-new, still in its Walmart box.

"What's this?" She stared at the mother and the baby photographed on the cover. "Wait . . ." She didn't get it at first. "What is this?"

"What do you mean?" He took it from her. "What are you doing? What are you looking for?"

"My sunglasses. I told you."

He put the monitor in his lap and moved his hand over the wheel again. She looked at his lap.

"A friend—some friends of ours are having a baby," he explained.

"What?"

"I don't know, Ellie. Marianne bought it. I guess there's a baby shower. That's what you women do, right? Have baby showers?"

"Right, we love those. I don't believe you."

"Okay." He pulled off the road beside the familiar ditch, the grass sunburned and thick like hemp. The start of the long driveway was a few feet away. She looked at it.

"Don't go yet," she said.

"I have to get back." He took his phone from his pocket and numbered his passcode. Had he always had a passcode? She looked over his shoulder as he read a text. Marianne had texted twice and called twice.

Ellie rolled her eyes. "Well, give me an idea, like a ballpark frame of when you're coming back."

"Why do you need a time? You hear my car—what else are you doing?"

"I like to have some warning." She liked looking forward to it, was the truth.

"Are you seeing someone?" he said. "Because it would be okay with me."

"Are you serious? Who would I see out here? Who would I meet?"

"I don't know—Rand?"

"It's Ran. And, are you fucking kidding me?"

"Why not?"

"*What?*"

"No, it's just—maybe you should see someone—you know, who's available. Maybe someone who's, you know, your age."

"Right, because you're just my married boyfriend."

"Well . . . yes."

She looked at him incredulously.

"If I wasn't married, we wouldn't be sitting here."

"So?"

"So, you wouldn't have wanted me otherwise. It would have been too involved for you. Too real. Being married made me safe. Now you're all . . . acting different."

"We wouldn't be sitting here if you had ever thought I *could* commit. You were just a conventional married person, and I was exciting to you. I was your excitement. But now, as soon as I offer you something real—"

"Honey, is that what you're doing? Come on. What does that even mean to you?"

She didn't reply.

"I'm flattered," he finally said, taking her hand. He clasped his fingers around it, then kissed the top of her knuckles. "I have so much on my plate right now."

Like that, his phone chimed with another text. He read it and wrote back quickly. The purple vein at his temple appeared, and the lines around his eyes deepened. He sighed. "I really have to head out."

"Why?"

"I'm late. I forgot about an appointment."

"What appointment?"

"Come on, Ellie."

She put her cup in the plastic bag of trash. He passed her the bottle. "It'll just sit around if I take it home. I'm trying to be healthier. I can't believe I just used that word with you."

"No, just forget it." She reached for her shirt in the backseat and caught her image in the side mirror. She felt ugly. Her eyes were red and small and watery. Her cheeks were pink with sun, and her forehead shone despite the drying-out rage of the AC.

"Friday. I'll come Friday." He looked at her. "Three o'clock, okay? I'll be in the same spot."

"Whatever."

She made sure her LUCKY YOU's were zipped. LUCKY YOU didn't even seem ironic now. Not ironic, and not sexy, either—just one of life's meaningless little stupidities.

She went around the car and stood at his window, inhaling the hot fumes from his engine. They held each other's wrists for a minute before she stepped back, and the window went up.

She watched him drive away.

She stood there after he'd disappeared, watching the road where he had been seconds ago.

· · ·

Rachel dealt cards for Egyptian Rat Screw in the shade of the back deck. They faced each other with their legs outstretched, the arches of their feet touching every now and then.

They flipped cards down, ready to slap royal marriages and doubles of spades and hearts while they talked intermittently about the Real World, which hung in the air like a question mark.

"I'm going to take up tennis I think," Rachel said. Little sweat pearls glistened above her lip.

"You told me." Ellie slapped the deck of cards a half second after Rachel. Too late. "Haven't you already taken up tennis? Here, I mean?"

"I want to play tennis for real. Two Jacks," Rachel said, showing her the match. Ellie collected the pile. "I used to play when I was little, you know," she said. They started again.

"You told me." Ellie said that she wanted two things when she got back to the Real World. "One," she said, straightening her hand, "is that I want to do something, find something that matters. And two, I don't want to live alone again."

"I *have* to live alone," Rachel insisted, "or I'm going to kill someone. God, to have my own room. I'm so sick of living with someone. I mean—not you," she said. She turned around and glanced at Autry under the tree. He was reading *Better Off*—a book by an MIT graduate who grew a beard, joined an Amish community, and lived without electricity for a year. Now he drove a rickshaw and made homemade soap in Missouri. This great mind—and he was making soap.

"He can't hear us," Ellie reassured her.

"You'd be surprised." Rachel studied her cards. "He's

always listening. He's paranoid about *everything*, it's weird."

"I don't think you understand how bad living alone can get. I mean, it can get *real* bad. You've always lived with a boyfriend, you don't know. There was the cyclist, before Autry. Before him, all through college, it was that British guy. Then—"

"All right, but see, you don't know how bad living with someone can get. You've never done it. You've never lived with someone that you can't stand. You don't know what it's like to truly hate someone. It's *hard*."

"I just get too crazy. I scare myself. Whatever happens, I'm not going to live alone again." The panic and anxiety and the fear of loneliness—she couldn't risk it. She couldn't risk the craziness.

"Who do you want to live with?" Rachel asked.

Ellie knew exactly who she was going to live with, but she wasn't ready to tell Rachel yet. She was struggling with some guilt just now. She could tell herself anything she wanted: *I'm* not married. *I'm* not betraying anyone. *I* didn't take any vows. It's *Michael's* problem. At the same time, she knew what she was doing was wrong, wasn't it, because otherwise she wouldn't have to keep justifying it in her head all the time.

"Do you want to live with *Ran*?" Rachel teased.

"Stop."

"Phoenix?"

"Phoenix Pace? Why would you say that?"

"You talk about him sometimes."

"I do?"

"He comes up when we do our ASMR talks."

"That's weird. But actually, it kind of makes sense. He does have this kind of deadening ASMR quality."

"He puts you to sleep?"

"Something like it."

"Really?"

"Yeah, like the undreaming kind. When you may as well be dead. We kissed once, a long time ago. He's like my brother."

"Like your brother in a good way, or a bad way?"

Ellie laughed. "Is there ever a *good* way?"

"Maybe if you have an incest fetish . . ."

"Stop," Ellie laughed. "Anyway, I think Phoenix might be gay, or bisexual."

"Maybe he's trisexual."

"What's trisexual?"

"When you'll try anything!"

"Everyone should be trisexual."

They talked more about changing their lives, the Real World. But the more they talked, the more they tried to pin the details, the more overwhelming and impossible it all seemed. What would they *do?*

"I just beat you," Rachel said.

Ellie looked down. Her hand was gone.

Ellie saw things being burned up in her head all week. She swam in the creek, played Egyptian Rat Screw or Hearts on the deck with Rachel, their legs outstretched, red ants going in and out of the boards under their thighs.

"Do you really think Ran will come back?" Rachel said.

Ellie thought of Ran and his girlfriend, how sweet they were together on that sunny rock across the water. "He's so decent in his own strange way, it makes me want to cry." Sometimes she just loved everyone and everything so much. She made herself think of something hateful to balance this out. She thought of Marianne. She thought of the baby monitor. There.

The baby monitor—had Michael *wanted* her to find it? What was that nonsense about a baby shower? She wondered if Marianne was really pregnant. Could she *really* be pregnant? *Pregnant* pregnant?

Mornings, they stared out from the back deck and read the weather, the purple mountains in the distance. She was waiting, waiting for Friday. Waiting for Michael. She felt him pulling away from her, and so she needed to light everything on fire Friday. She was going to tell him that she was ready to welcome him into her real life.

She paced.

She paced and read haikus, waiting for the heat to break.

She paced.

"Listen to this one," Ellie told Rachel, watering a row of wilted leeks. "It's going to require your full attention."

Rachel held the green watering can at her hip and looked at her. The water came from the rain barrel, and it smelled bad.

"Escaped the nets— / escaped the ropes— / moon on the water."

Rachel was still. "Is that it?"

"Well. What do you mean?"

"Oh—I like it."

"Listen to another one." She turned the page.

She and Rachel slept with cold washcloths on their foreheads, side by side on the kitchen floor, the coolest place in the house. Autry sat up meditating in the great room, counting dead flies on the floor.

Earlier, he wandered into the kitchen and asked, "What does your face look like before your mother and father were born?" They stared at him, then looked at each other.

By the time Ellie would start to drift to sleep, the washcloth would warm to her forehead. So they took turns getting up to rewet the washcloths with cold water.

One night she dreamed that she was back at the Bio-Life Plasma donation center. Only instead of donating her own insides, she was a technician, marking her clipboard, wearing the thin white lab coat, and Marianne Lindsey was the donor. Marianne was pregnant, her stomach inflated like a basketball, lying with her right arm extended for Ellie.

Instead of finding her vein, or a side vein, Ellie put the needle in her stomach, over her clothes, and let the air out.

Rachel said her relationship with Autry was over, essentially, Autry just didn't know it. "We don't sleep together anymore. I miss the orgasms—it's not quite the same when you have to do it yourself."

"Yeah," Ellie said.

"Then again, I don't know, after a while, it seems even an orgasm only goes so far."

"At some point, with the wrong person, you'd rather just be reading or something."

Rachel said he was most recently working up chapter title

ideas about how to square dance and other ways to have fun in health. Charades, for example, and games involving string.

Every time he'd come up with a new title, or section title, he asked Ellie and Rachel about it. He was obsessed with titles and section titles. Ellie thought about how Ran hadn't cared what they called his lip balm.

"In truth, health; in health, truth," Autry said, after the Keats line. "What do you think about that for an alternate book title?"

Ellie and Rachel exchanged a glance, a shrug. "Maybe," Ellie said.

"No," Rachel said.

"At least for a section title."

Every now and then, when they would play cards on the deck, he would come outside and stand around them naked. "It's the only way I can get to the truth," he explained. "Stripped, it's a metaphor."

Ellie wondered if he was really starting to lose it.

Ellie tried to remember what she herself had ever found cool about him. She couldn't think of anything. All that surfaced was that Rachel had once found him cool, and so he had been cool.

On Thursday, she and Rachel were playing cards on the deck when they heard an engine—a distant rumbling at first, like weather.

They looked up.

It wasn't Friday—it was Thursday, Ellie reminded herself again. So it couldn't be Michael. It was still morning. It couldn't even be three o'clock. The sun was hidden behind a negative of clouds. The day was white with humidity, without a shadow. Time was erasing itself as the engine came closer.

"Autry's parents," Rachel said, looking at Ellie.

It had not stopped at the bottom of the driveway, in the weeds—her cue—as Michael would have done.

"Ran?"

But it wasn't the sound Ran's truck made. Plus, he always slowed down at the bottom of the driveway, so he didn't kick up gravel dust.

They shaded their eyes with their hands and listened.

Something big and gold was in the driveway now, moving toward the house. Rachel squinted.

Ellie swallowed.

She saw Marianne's blond head in the windshield, over the wheel, then Michael beside her, in the passenger seat. He did not look at Ellie or Rachel as Marianne pulled up to them. She stopped the car abruptly; the brakes made their heads tilt slightly forward, in sync.

Ellie watched Marianne lean over the gear shift and said something to Michael. Then she stepped out, leaving her door open, with the *ding ding ding ding* going. Michael reached over and took the keys out of the ignition. He went around to her side, slowly, and shut the door behind her.

Ellie stared as Marianne approached the back deck in a summer-white maternity tunic. Her stomach was round and her arms were thin and tanned and now Ellie could not pretend otherwise: They were having a baby. She walked over the grass in her heels, with Michael following behind her. He wouldn't look at Ellie.

Michael stood behind her. "Hello," Marianne said. When she opened her mouth to speak, Ellie saw the condition of her teeth—they were gray, the enamel worn off. "We're going to make this quick."

Ellie looked at Michael, but Michael looked at the ground again, then at Marianne's back.

"Michael has something he'd like to tell you," she said, her voice flat and steady with rage. She turned toward him, but he didn't say anything.

Nobody said anything.

"I know you were expecting Michael, not me," Marianne went on. "I know everything. I know when he comes here. I'm not stupid."

"I . . . don't know," Ellie said, shaking her head. She stared at the edges of the trees in front of her. She wanted to clip the tree line, to make it even.

"What—you don't know what? You don't know that you're a slut? I'm sorry—what is it you don't you know?"

"Mare—" Michael said.

"Oh, great," Rachel said. "A woman calling another woman a slut. Just what we need."

Marianne continued as if she hadn't heard. "You didn't think this could go on forever, did you?" She laughed through her nose. "You didn't think Michael was really interested in sluts, in whores, in dirty girls—"

"Oh, good lord!" Rachel exclaimed. She nearly laughed.

Ellie didn't want to believe these words could touch her, but they did. She felt them down her chest as if she'd swallowed something she would never really be able to forget. She cleared her throat.

"I *love* my husband," Marianne said.

"Okay?" Ellie said.

"Just let it go," Michael whispered, taking Marianne's hand.

Marianne whirled around, and yanked her arm away. "Say what you're going to say," she told him. She turned to Ellie now. "He wants to tell you something. My husband has something to say to you."

Michael's tie was loosened at his neck, his face unshaven. "All right," he said. "Marianne is pregnant, and if we're going to do this, I need to stop seeing you. All right. There. Come on, let's go." He turned to Marianne. "Did we really have to come all the way out here for that?"

"No, no, no. You're not doing it for me," Marianne said. "And you're not doing it just because I'm pregnant . . ."

"Okay." He took a deep breath, "Okay. I regret everything, it was all a mistake, I don't know what I was thinking, and we have to end this relationship now. Okay." He looked at the sky. "Now, let's go. All right?"

She looked at Ellie. "Did you think I didn't know?"

"I'm just living my life," Ellie said. "I don't know about your issues and problems. I'm not married to you."

"Do you think he ever cared about you? There have been plenty of girls just like you. But now we're starting a family . . ."

Michael sighed painfully. "Mare, look, you made your point, now let's go—she understands."

"I knew you would do this," Marianne said.

"Do what?" he asked flatly.

"Back home, earlier today, you were *crying*, *begging*, on your *knees*, begging me to let you stay, because you want to be a father so much, begging me to let you raise this baby . . . 'Oh, I'll do anything,' you begged. 'Don't leave me, don't leave me, don't leave me . . .'"

Ellie stared at him, hating him now. "We've never been more than just friends," Ellie said.

Marianne nodded—this was what she'd wanted to hear.

"How far along are you?" Ellie asked.

Marianne touched her stomach. "Five months."

"Really?" Rachel said. "You look unhealthy for five months."

Marianne stared at her.

"Small," Rachel clarified.

"That's because he makes her throw up," Ellie said. "They're both sick people . . . I don't want anything to do with either of them ever again."

"Why would you want to add another human being to this already overpopulated planet?" Rachel added.

Michael shook his head. "Let's go. Come on, let's go. I told you, honey—they're crazy. Didn't I tell you?"

"I'm *not* crazy," Ellie said. "And neither is Rachel."

Marianne took Michael's arm, and they turned around to leave.

"Wait," Ellie said.

They both turned around, but it was Michael who stepped back toward her.

"Wait," she said again. "Wait . . ."

He looked right into her eyes now. He moved a strand from her braid behind her ear. "Oh, Ellie," he said.

She looked beyond him, at the trees, so she wouldn't start crying. She looked back at him. He wiped a tear from her face. "We're married," he said, softly. "If I want this life, if I want to be a good father . . . I mean, I can't . . ."

"But you're unhappy."

"She's my *wife*."

"He—he regrets everything," Marianne interjected. "He said you were just some stupid girl he felt sorry for."

"Please, stop," Michael said.

"He said that you were a talentless drunk."

That one hurt.

"It's over. Isn't that enough?" Michael said.

Autry was back then, walking out from the trail that wound behind the house. His T-shirt was wet from creek water.

"Ah," Michael said under his breath. "This moron." They glared at each other.

"Who the fuck are you?" Autry said. He was stoned. "Who is this?" Autry said, looking at Rachel.

"Let's go," Michael said. "Come on." He helped Marianne into the car, into the passenger seat now. She looked dead ahead, exhausted, like the outing had taken every ounce of her energy.

Ellie watched Michael walk to the driver's side. She could hear herself breathing now, as he turned the key in the ignition. The engine started. He turned the car around, then made the turn at the end of the driveway. She watched until they were gone. A violent emptiness took over, a brutal vacant space; it was almost pleasant.

YOUR TENNIS PRO BOYFRIEND

RACHEL

OCTOBER 2009

Rachel's boyfriend stood across the net at the hopper, feeding balls to her backhand. He was yelling, *Down the line . . . crosscourt . . . down the line . . . crosscourt . . .* She hit them back *down the line, crosscourt, down the line . . .*

Except she lofted a few over his head, and a few fell into the sun-filled net, its shadow crocheted along the center of the court like a second net. Whenever she noticed it, she hit balls into it.

So she tried to think of nothing, like Hardin said. Just blink and hit. But before she could *get* to the not-thinking phase, she had to think of nothing *but* strokes and angles, percentages and footwork. Eventually, she wouldn't have to think. Her movements would begin to feel as natural as movement itself.

Sometimes this seemed confusing, but Hardin had this way of explaining everything. She was getting better every day, he said, and he'd know, because he was USTA ranked once.

He had a patent on a new grip—one with raised grooves to help beginners transition from backhand to forehand and back. She could listen to him talk about the differences between Western and Continental all night.

After every stroke—down the line . . . *thwock* . . . crosscourt . . . *thwock* . . . down the line . . . *thwock*—she shook her bangs from her eyes. When she moved back to Fayetteville, she went to Nesbit: The Salon for Changes for thick, blunt bangs. The fact that they were already growing out was comforting—like nothing was final. No drastic haircut, no decision, no one mistake. Nothing was the end of her. She was raging with invincibility.

In the mirror, a new girl looked back, her eyes electric with desire and ambition. She blinked.

Just blink and hit.

She spent money she didn't have on white Nike skirts with

tiny white shorts. She wore colored contacts that turned her eyes into blue skies. She painted her toes vermillion and burgundy and crushed purple.

She was running up a credit card, but this was all an investment. She had the growing suspicion, anyway, that everyone had debt, even the richest members of the club. Especially the richest, she wanted to think.

The only piece of her that still looked like the old Rachel—Ray—was the sunspot under her eye, which had settled into a tan scar on her face. She said it was a birthmark.

After the lesson, they picked up. Hardin rolled the hopper into the shed, and she watched him through the metal fence, over the water bottle at her lips.

They rode their bikes home, dead leaves blowing around their tires as they pedaled downhill toward the pro house, where they lived together.

Four pros lived in the pro house. The ceiling in Hardin's attic bedroom slanted down sharply so she hit her head, walking around the brown IKEA nightstand with *Maxim* magazines on it. Nails on the wall held tennis hats that used to be white, and racquets to hit through the seasons. The TV turned the room shades of blue, while reruns of *Family Guy* and *The Big Bang Theory* played all afternoon to no one.

The pros complained that the washer and dryer were too eco-friendly. "It takes a fucking hour to wash whites. Then they're not even white. Then an hour to dry them . . ." The dryer used a third of the energy a regular dryer used. "It's bullshit," Hardin said.

Rachel totally agreed.

Before she'd started taking lessons, Hardin dated the divorced women and single moms he gave lessons to, helping them with their serves, explaining the math of doubles. Whenever she teased him about it, he smiled and turned shy. Rachel wanted them gone.

One pro stayed at his girlfriend's place. Another pro liked the bars, and some mornings a girl with cloudy makeup under her eyes would be drowning in one of his T-shirts, eating cereal and looking for an outlet to charge her phone.

Christine was the fourth pro—cropped blond hair like Martina Navratilova's and sun-dark skin. Rachel studied her, because Christine was once in Autry's circle. They used to hike, apparently, and play ultimate Frisbee, before Rachel knew Autry.

Every time this Christine walked through the living room, visor around her neck, the intersection happened. She didn't want to be on nodding terms with any of her former selves. It made the world feel small. She worried, sometimes desperately worried, that all her previous lives were going to catch up with her.

Oh, thank god for Hardin. The only life that mattered, she told herself, was the one she was living now.

She was late for work again. If only she didn't have to work, she thought. If only she could stay home watching TV with Hardin, planted in the living room's blue glare. With her head in his lap, she'd pull the image from the TV around his half-full

Bud Light. They might get stoned and walk to the grocery store, and put a frozen DiGiorno on Rachel's credit card.

Last night they ate "taco bell"—crunchy Doritos-flavored taco shells with bright yellow cheese. She forgot who she was for a second, and went off on the quality of Taco Bell meat: "A recent study shows that taco bell meat is only one grade higher than dog meat."

Hardin looked at her. "So?"

"Oh, yeah," she said. "No, I mean, yeah. I was just saying. It tastes good."

"It tastes great."

They made fun of the dreadlocked college kids walking to Edible Landscape. Hardin said the only reason people went to college was to avoid getting a job.

"Maybe I'll come see you at work tonight," Hardin suggested.

She loved when Hardin came to Viceroy. She loved so many things about him, just so many. But tonight, she had to see to some old business.

"I'm working with a friend I haven't seen in forever," Rachel said. "I need to catch up with her afterward."

Actually, her nerves were running like a dripping tap. What would Chloe *look* like? She wished she didn't have to be reminded of the Ozark house so soon, but this was Fayetteville, and everybody saw everybody saw everybody saw everybody in Fayetteville.

"Ya'll are going out?" he asked.

"No, god no. We'll just have a shift drink together."

He was still wearing his white tennis hat. She liked that he wore it backward when he wasn't on-court. She kissed him, then wheeled her bike through the door.

She pedaled through the wind, past the new coffeehouse where tiny bulbs burned on long wires. She passed the grocery store marquee, where the *y* in YOUR had fallen from the word, so instead of reading OPEN TIL 9 FOR YOUR CONVENIENCE, it read OPEN TIL 9 FOR OUR CONVENIENCE. She would love to text Ellie a picture of this. But she wasn't ready. She needed time to completely step out of her old soul and into this new one before she could reveal herself to anyone.

She'd had no contact with Autry since the afternoon his parents had flown up, after she and Ellie had finally called them from Ran's cell phone. It took them only a week to take care of everything. Autry went back with his parents to Texas. He was living with them now, working for his dad, studying the Alexander Technique and interested in Scientology.

How could she have loved that person!

She would never feel that way about Hardin.

She was crazy about Hardin.

Viceroy had even more day drinkers now, fewer students. The 86 list was always long, even though they weren't busy. Bartenders picked up cranberry juice and cans of Coke and ginger ale, because Bruce and Lorraine still hadn't fixed the guns. Bruce was more demanding than before, but cared less.

"One of you left the scoop in the ice cream last night," he told Rachel when she walked in the kitchen. "Now it's frozen there."

"I wasn't working last night."

"It was the new girl, then. What difference does it make? Someone deal with it."

Rachel looked out the kitchen cutout window at the new girl, wearing black cutoffs over distressed Nancy Spungen fishnet hose. The new girl and the new girl's friend, the *other* new girl, were twenty, and saving money to move to either Austin or Chicago. They talked about it like they were the first people to think of this. They didn't understand that everyone who had ever worked at Viceroy was, at some point, moving to Austin or Chicago.

Then Rachel saw her: Chloe, tying on her apron. Her weight gain was startling, her hair growing out to her shoulders. She looked normal; she looked healthy.

"We need more salads," Bruce told Rachel.

Rachel didn't think they needed more salads, so she stood around.

"Chloe's back to work tonight, huh," Bruce said. He was chopping vegetables, lost in the contradiction of concentration and absentmindedness.

"Yeah, it's cool," Rachel said, wishing she meant it.

"Ever hear from Ellie?"

"No."

"She picked up a check here," Bruce said.

"You told me."

"Never to be heard from again. She's a vanishing act."

Lorraine entered from the landing off the kitchen, and Rachel had always been a little afraid of her, so she decided to make salads, after all.

Lorraine mixed the house, shaking its purple ingredients in huge plastic containers, while Rachel placed wedges of tomatoes on each plate, then sprinkled shredded carrots and cabbage over the wilted romaine. They would probably throw these salads away at the end of the night.

Who cared?

She had to learn to quit thinking about wasted food. It was a worry that belonged to a former Rachel. To prove she could waste food, she dropped a tomato wedge on the floor and left it there. There.

Lorraine wore frayed jeans and a white T-shirt with different colored parted lips all over it. Bruce watched her walk to the front, through the door's cutout window.

"What a fucking bitch," Bruce said.

Rachel pretended not to hear.

Lorraine was dating a twenty-seven-year-old accountant she'd met online. He drove a Versa with a Bush '04 bumper sticker.

Hardin, in fact, had voted for Bush. Twice.

But that was just one of those things, wasn't it? Look, it wasn't as though she and Hardin were ever going to discuss politics, or anything else that mattered. The idea of having a serious conversation with Hardin made her smile.

Bruce was dating a bartender from Que Sera. She was twenty-eight with dyed black hair and mascara that collected in the corner of her eyes. Lorraine was adamant that she was ugly. Bruce insisted to Lorraine that, very soon, her boyfriend would be fat.

Sometimes they brought them here, these people, to make each other jealous in front of everyone.

"How's your tennis-pro boyfriend?" Bruce asked Rachel.

"Perfect."

"Perfect," Bruce repeated, imitating her.

"He is," Rachel replied. "He's perfection."

Rachel went around all shift with *your tennis-pro boyfriend* in her head. It had this great ring to it.

She waited on a group of Walmart shareholders, who were thoroughly unimpressed with the food and her service. They tipped her twenty percent, but made her feel like an idiot first. At least it wasn't the weekend—Rachel hated serving the middle-aged cowboy-boot-wearing dancing drunks.

Chloe and Rachel traded smiles all through the shift, but didn't speak. They avoided each other all night in the dark spaces where you reach for ice and pint glasses with logos of breweries on them. They avoided going to the walk-in freezer in the basement.

Finally the neon OPEN flickered to CLOSED. They ran their server reports, the printer running out of ink, and poured shift drinks. Rachel's shift drink was only about the ritual— she liked that the night was over. She poured herself a draft of hard cider, which tasted like chilled apple juice. Chloe drank tequila, then Coke.

They rolled flatware at the card table in the basement. Bruce's shirts hung on wire hangers, swaying under the vents like slow dancers. A mouse flashed across the aisle.

Lamplight picked out the dyed-blond streaks in Chloe's hair—no bald places. Her collarbone was flat inside her body, her cheeks filled out.

Music drifted down the steps, and they talked about bands and Obama, so normal that it really wasn't normal. They talked about Natalie's, because Jim had a residency at Natalie's every Monday night.

Crush Heat Burn had broken up. Jim was a one-man band, Chloe said proudly. He had recorded the songs he wrote at Autry's. "He doesn't have to travel as much now," Chloe said. "Except when he wants to. And then I usually go with him."

"Well," Rachel said. "You look stunning. What's your secret?"

Chloe stared back blankly. "I'm seeing a therapist."

"And that's good? What do you guys talk about?"

"We don't talk. He just writes me prescriptions. Look at my face right now." Rachel looked at her face. "I'm practically asleep—isn't that amazing?" Chloe smiled, then looked down at the fork and knife she was wrapping into the linen like a Chinese doll.

"Do you *want* to be asleep?"

Chloe looked at her. "You know? I'm so content. I'm so happy. And you know what? I can't cry. Like I literally, physically, am unable to cry."

"That's terrible."

"No, it's gorgeous. I feel so stable."

Chloe and Jim lived in the studio above Natalie's. Rachel had never known Chloe to be so talkative. She had always been the listener. Now it was the other way around.

They heard Bruce's shoes coming down the steps. "Girl talk," Bruce exclaimed happily. "What are we dishing about?"

When they didn't respond, he said, "You don't have to quit talking about me just because I'm here." He stood in front of them and changed his shirt, slowly. "I'm just kidding," he said. "Jesus. Lighten up."

Rachel and Chloe went on marrying the forks and knives.

"Where are you headed tonight, Bruce?" Rachel asked out of politeness.

"Going to see the lady at Que Sera."

When he was gone, they heard the dregs of his fight with Lorraine drift down the stairs.

Chloe said, "I'm surprised Bruce hasn't found Ellie, wherever she is. I'm sure his torch still burns for her."

They both laughed a little. But Chloe's laugh was stale and forced—the motion of laughing without laughing.

"This place," Rachel said. "I'm so tired of it already. Again."

"I could probably work here forever. It works for me, it works for Jim." She yawned. "I'm in love I guess."

If that was being in love, Rachel thought—yawning and antidepressants—then never mind. "Does Ellie know?"

"Know what?"

"That you and Jim live together?"

"Oh. I don't know," Chloe replied. "Would she care? I feel bad, sometimes, that things got weird between us. I don't know if I was wrong, or if she was wrong, or if I'm right to feel . . . I don't know. What do you think?"

"You're both right, you're both wrong."

"Well. What about you?" Chloe asked.

Rachel told her about tennis, about Hardin, but didn't extend details beyond that.

Chloe strayed from one thread of conversation to the next, until all the silverware was rolled into a pyramid.

Rachel had been ready to apologize for anything, but they never mentioned the Ozark house, or the Project.

Rachel unwound the cord of the vacuum cleaner and vacuumed the upstairs carpet. She let its loud suck erase her past. The future, they all said, belonged to those who could see it. She pushed the vacuum back and forth over the carpet. Its vibrations were in her shoes. She kept pushing the future into the carpet.

She biked home to her tennis-pro boyfriend, the red safety light blinking from her handlebars. She walked the bike inside and leaned it into place against the wall, beside Christine's Prince bag. The house was asleep. She untied her shoes and slouched in the kitchen chair. Mail littered the table, with bananas going brown, sets of keys, two racquets. She shuffled through the envelopes with her name on them. Whenever CHASE or WELLS FARGO glared at her, panic rang, just barely, with a heartbeat through her ears.

She didn't like to open bills, but she opened one anyway, from her dentist. Three hundred eighty dollars to Dr. Sterling for filling a cavity.

When she returned to Fayetteville, she felt the greatest desire to get her teeth cleaned, and she loved it when people's last names corresponded to their profession.

She didn't have dental insurance. She didn't have health insurance.

It bothered her that they'd found her at the pro house. It wasn't as though she'd filled out an official change-of-address form. She'd lived in a room near Wilson Park until she moved in with Hardin, gradually—a suitcase here, a suitcase there.

She didn't *have* to pay this bill for $380, did she? She looked at her student loan bill in the stack, but didn't open it. She took everything else with her name printed in the window, and put it in the trash. She put her hands on top of the paper to sink the trash further into itself.

She did sit-ups to forget about money.

One day, she would have money—money to pay everything off, even her student loans. But if she never paid them off—so what? People lived with debt and died with debt, didn't they? They couldn't garnish your wages or come after you if you were dead.

She did sit-ups until her stomach tightened with fatigue, then push-ups.

She went upstairs, and stepped into a hot shower, which filled the mirrors with steam. For a long time, she let water rush down her body. There were times, in the shower, when she'd forget she was in the shower. Suddenly she would blink, thinking, *have I already washed my hair?* and honestly not know the answer.

When she was through, she waved her hand across the face of the mirror and regarded herself without feeling, trying to see herself clearly, as objectively as possible. It was difficult.

Eventually she climbed into bed still wearing her towel, wet hair against her back. She leaned against Hardin's body, and he squeezed her back in his dream. He mumbled something she didn't understand. She studied him until he sighed and whispered, "How was your shift?"

"Oh, good, you're awake now," she said, propping herself on one elbow. "Let's do something crazy."

"Mmm," he said, sleepy.

"Let's do something crazy," she repeated.

He turned to her and slipped a lazy hand between her thighs.

"Not that. We have to make sure we're alive, you know?"

He rubbed his eyes. "I know I'm alive."

"How do you know?"

He took her hand and moved it under the covers. God, she loved that he was practically always hard.

"Can we hit tomorrow?" she asked. She kissed him suddenly. "Let's hit for a long time."

"Sure." He touched her wet hair. "What's wrong, Rach?"

"What if we're just idiot robots, with no souls, being controlled by some outside force? What if we're just, like, medicated zombies?"

"What?" he said, sitting up a little, so his head was propped against a pillow in the dark. He was trying so hard to be interested, but it was as if he thought she were being cute. As if all she needed was to calm down. But she didn't want to calm down. She never wanted to calm down.

They kissed, and reached for each other. It was good, what happened next, but not like it was with Autry. It wasn't quite the same, Hardin's tongue. He would never just commit to a rhythm. But, still—she liked it, she liked it.

They sat on the bench after playing a set, their knees touching and parting and touching. She wasn't working tonight; they could play all night if they wanted, while the moths flurried around the lights and the evening hung the sky with stars.

"You're heatin' up," he said.

Meaning she played well.

She blushed.

They watched the games going on around them. One court was dotted with men in whites playing doubles, moving like chess pieces to the net, then back, to the baseline, then back.

On another court, a pretty blonde served to a tall man with silver hair. He returned it to her backhand. She sliced it, then went to net, the ruffles on her skirt accentuating the thinness of her legs. The woman, Rachel realized, was Marianne Lindsey, that woman who came to the house.

She saw her with this man often enough not to be jolted into surprise. There had always been something familiar about her, but she'd never consciously put it together until this moment. It made her nerves drip. Another reminder. Rachel watched them. *Thwock. Thwock.* Then Marianne hit a winner.

Had Michael and Marianne separated? She and this old man—were they together? She never saw Michael here.

Rachel doubted Marianne recognized her. If she did, she gave nothing away. This seemed to be the way things were handled here, in general. There existed a law of non-acknowledgment of certain things. Divorces and affairs, for example. Poverty. Death.

Waiting at the fence for Marianne was a much older woman pushing a stroller back and forth. So. She'd had the baby and everything.

Rachel watched Marianne serve wide. Her second serve was safe, and he returned it deep. Marianne played safe, Rachel saw, but she was consistent.

"Did you ever sleep with her?" Rachel asked Hardin. "You know, pre-me?"

He squinted in the direction Rachel was looking, at Marianne, and shook his head. "Too skinny." The wind blew, and a few leaves rushed across the courts. The ground was hardening with autumn. Birds were disappearing. The sun was cooling even as the children ran around under it in their tennis whites, playing Red Light/Green Light. Soon the bubble would go over the courts.

Soon she would get good enough to become a teaching pro. She could do it. She was still young—she was. She was twenty-five. She could do anything.

Playing tennis, becoming a pro—this was her thing. This was what she was onto. She would always be onto something. She would keep stepping over the bodies of the dead Rachels into the present Rachel. She would never settle down.

There would always be the *next* next thing, anyway, if tennis didn't work out. But it would, though. It would.

She could do anything she put her mind to, Hardin told

her, and she went around with this in her head all day every day like a prayer or mantra. This was the mantra by which she lived and died. These were the demons and gods that ruled her.

PLAY DEAD

ELLIE

FEBRUARY 2010

She had organized her life into a brick house on Diane
Lane with black shutters and a red front door with a
wreath, and a doorbell underneath the wreath. In front
was a greenish-brown lawn like a welcome mat.

Diane Lane—like the actress. Ellie wanted to text Rachel
a picture of the street sign and write, *I live here!* But she was
friendless just now.

That was all right.

It was easier this way, not to give anything away, not to reveal yourself to anyone.

Besides, she liked living with Phoenix. They did things together, like go to the grocery store. With a list, and everything. They watched Netflix in sweatpants and wool socks with holes in the heels. They cooked stir-fry and sloppy pastas and sealed the leftovers in Tupperware.

Weekends, they slept late, while sun burned through the windows, painting more windows on the rug. Phoenix and his friends might sit around the vaporizer playing Cards Against Humanity, or they'd watch movies where serious actors blow up buildings and drive cars with butterfly doors.

Phoenix and his friends liked to hike, and take drugs at electronic music shows. They liked Frisbee, and they threw the disc back and forth in the yard, over the frozen pools in the grass. As for Ellie, she didn't want to hike. She didn't want to listen to music, or be moved by beauty, or throw a Frisbee. She didn't want to camp under the stars or go to shows, even though Natalie's was booking residencies now, and campaigning for a roots festival.

The faintest thread of a lyric in her head—*Oh, I'll twine with my mingles and waving black hair*—or the tune of a murder ballad, or the two-step of a love song, all made her heart twist—dangerous—and she immediately replaced it with something superficial. Books and good movies and alcohol and art, except the playful, shallow kind, just made her feel things, so she quit them.

Besides, she didn't *want* to drink with Phoenix. She didn't want to feel turned on, in any sense of the word. It was so much easier, so much safer, not to let yourself feel anything.

Oh, she'd have a few beers. But they only made her sleepy. She felt connected to their cat. She liked to smoke weed, and feel her muscles melt into the sofa. She understood the appeal of weed now.

Boxes of notebooks and haikus collected dust under her bed. Her stuffed dogs stayed in boxes. She packed her mind-space with apps and Twitter and Facebook—*You have one new friend request*—and YouTube. *You can skip this advertisement in five seconds.* Image, image, image. *Upgrade now.* Swipe. Delete. Like. Like, Like, Like.

They fell asleep while the TV's color played across the comforter, across their arms and eyelids. *Record this. Demand it. Are you sure you want to delete? You cannot undo this action.* Sometimes it was difficult to discern real life: Was real life happening in real time, or was real life the life on all the screens? Her thoughts were filled with the images of screen-life.

They dressed for work in the morning while a reality show repeated its episode in the background: *I'm not here to make friends!* She watched enough reality television that sometimes she, herself, had the sensation of being filmed.

"That's because we *are* being filmed," Phoenix reminded her, pointing to the surveillance cameras that recorded and played them—to who?—as they walked down the street past the chain of bars, the jewelry store with its rings in the front window, the bookstore, the restaurant patios with wrought-iron furniture and strings of lights, the Walmart Supercenter.

On Monday morning, Phoenix dropped her off at Fayetteville Montessori School, where she worked as a teaching assistant in a classroom of four- to seven-year-olds. The SUVs waited like a long dark necklace in the horseshoe drop-off loop.

Then Phoenix drove to work, where he—well, she didn't know what he did, exactly, and she couldn't ask again. Her mind just drifted when he started to talk.

But it went something like this: If a company—Great Value, for example, a Walmart brand—wanted to make a new design for its individually packaged cakes—a Christmas swirl at Christmas, let's say—then Phoenix's company would build the machine to make the swirl atop the cake. He was taking classes again, too, but she forgot which ones.

Once again it had been hard finding a job, and she refused to return to Viceroy. She found the Montessori job posted on Craigslist. She had no childcare experience, but she lied her way through an interview, and they were short for assistants. She studied the Method, and passed the test. She was lucky.

She walked around the fluorescent room while the real teacher read aloud from a book about hurricanes, the eye and its system of categories. Strung up on the cinderblock walls were paper snowflakes and self-portraits done on construction paper, dolphin anatomy and maps of coral reefs.

At recess, she stood shivering in the yard with her hands in a pair of knitted gloves. Wind blew the flags and rattled the chains against the poles. She watched the children dip down the slide. Now and then, a little girl would run up and hug

Ellie's legs, then tighten her scarf and run away again. This nearly broke her heart.

Birds perched in the trees above the swings. Birds were nice. The class put seed in the feeders, and filled the empty flowerpots with water for baths.

It turned out Ellie liked children—who knew?—but she wasn't effective as a teaching assistant. She was no disciplinarian, and the kids knew it.

That was all right. She wasn't the *real* teacher.

She and Phoenix texted throughout the day: *How's your day going? Good. Yours? Good. What do you want to do for dinner? Pizza? Cool.* Emoji.

They ate Hawaiian pizza in front of a reality show about prisoners doing life. Criminals walked around in orange jumpsuits, talking to the camera with cell bars in the background.

"Please just come," Phoenix was saying.

He watched the screen. She watched the screen. She wiped her mouth with a napkin.

Walmart was—well, she hadn't exactly been listening, but from what she pieced together, Walmart was hosting a dinner on Saturday night for the local companies they worked with. Or something like that.

She didn't want to go. Michael's and Marianne's faces floated in her brain like dolls' heads. Of course, they would be there. Or worse—they wouldn't. She'd work herself up for nothing, then be crushed by their absence. "You'll have more fun without me," she said. "I don't act right at parties."

"What do you mean? You're great at parties. It's not a party, anyway, it's a dinner."

"Oh. I'll act even worse."

"Come on."

"I have nothing to wear."

"What about that green dress hanging in the closet, with the long sleeves? It's beautiful, and I've never seen it on you."

Phoenix's outfit was already hanging from the hook on the door—a smart suit his mother bought him.

"*You* should go—you go." Pineapples and cheese were starting to confuse each other, but she took another bite.

"Like everyone is bringing their wife or husband—or, you know, whatever, their partner. It's a thing. It's a thing people just do. It's called being an adult," he said tenderly, putting his arm around her. "Think about it. Okay?"

She put her head on his shoulder and looked at the television. They watched the men in orange outfits.

"The afternoon lesson tomorrow in school is on haikus," she offered.

"You told me. Do you want to read some? Where is that book you used to have?"

"I think I have alcohol dementia," she said. "I repeat myself."

"What?"

"I repeat myself."

"What?"

"I repeat—I get it." She laughed a little. It was funny that Phoenix could make her laugh, when actually she was dead.

At least the depression was steady—a constant. It was

comforting, in a way—like not getting out of bed, or not having to speak for hours at a time. She could hide in it and no one could find her.

She was fond of Phoenix, though, she was. It wasn't his fault. She appreciated his neatness, for example, his competence, his dedication to hygiene, his ability to wear clothes that fit.

As a couple, they posed threats to no one. She felt it in people's approving smiles as they pushed their cart down the grocery aisle, wheels squeaking, or when he dropped her off at work—*Bye!*—or when they strolled through the pedestrian mall with their huge coffees, looking in the storefront windows.

It wasn't like being with Michael, when people would look at them like something was slightly off. Their intimacy was disturbing, in a way (and the intimacy was obvious, she realized now): his wedding ring, the age difference. She remembered the way his other assistants treated her.

It wasn't like being with Jim, either—where her desire and pride in him overwhelmed and alarmed people.

With Phoenix, everything was normal. They were that normal couple buying groceries at the grocery store, doing the everyday. *That's* what people wanted. That's what they liked to see.

Ellie wrapped the leftover pizza slices in plastic, then placed them in Tupperware and collapsed the box the pizza came in, near the other cardboard boxes. On Thursday, the cardboard boxes went to the curb. She enjoyed the monotony of these kinds of routines. Trash, recycling, mail—it was mind-numbing and comforting.

They undressed for bed with their backs to each other, but brushed their teeth side by side in the mirror. Phoenix made faces at her; she smiled back at him through the mirror, then spit into the sink.

"I'll go," she said.

"You'll go?" Blue paste gurgled down the drain. He looked at her. "Really?" He hugged her, the brush still in his mouth.

Oh, she'd go to this party with him. Dinner. Whatever it was.

They turned the bedroom TV to the prisoners. Color flashed over the comforter from the images. When they turned down the bed, movement flashed over the sheets. They pulled the sheet over them, then the comforter. She followed the line of orange jumpsuits from their cells to the prison yard, a square of concrete outlined in some grass, then to their beds. She thought about the nature of prison.

The credits rolled, and she thought about the word *comforter*, how it was a thing instead of a person—and this got mixed up in a dream shifting just under her thoughts, which is when she felt him on her back, trying to have sex with her.

She could pretend to be asleep, or she could go with it.

She turned her body around. She used a vibrator with Phoenix, and that was all right—it was easier this way, just to do it yourself. He was inside her, then he wasn't, then he straddled her and masturbated with his eyes closed until he came on her chest.

She looked down at her chest.

That was all right.

He sighed, then exploded with laughter. All right. This urge to laugh after sex was common in men, except Phoenix's laughter was unsettling, as if he were laughing *at* her—as if he'd just conquered something she had nothing to do with.

He propped himself on an elbow. "Here, it's good for your skin," he said, spreading his semen over her décolletage, where faint, tiny lines had appeared. "You know I'll still love you? Even when you have wrinkles."

She wanted to fall into a death-deep sleep. But they watched TV again, his arm around her. She reminded herself that she was lucky. She was comfortable. She was safe. This was life, she supposed. This was a thing people did. This was how people lived.

They'd had a talk—*the* talk—not long after they'd started living together, when Ellie moved back to Fayetteville. She'd stayed with Ran and his girlfriend at first, until she found the Montessori job and arranged her life with Phoenix.

Phoenix told her that he was a little bisexual, about seventy-thirty. Seventy percent interested in women, thirty percent men.

He wanted a life with a woman though, he assured Ellie. That was definitely the life he wanted—though he might occasionally have sex with men while they were together.

Well, that was all right.

They talked frequently about the complexities of sexuality. They debated the attractiveness of people on TV. Would you have sex with her? Would you have sex with him?

Gay or straight, bisexual or trisexual, what she knew for sure now—and actually what did not even matter to her, anymore—was that they were sexually incompatible. Irrevocably incompatible.

During the day, if she thought about them touching, she felt queasy. That was all right. There was more to life than touch, wasn't there? *Wasn't* there?

It was safer this way, to be in control, not to want. Desire only caused problems in the end.

At school the next morning, Ellie listened as the real teacher taught the haiku lesson. She used American examples. Some were patriotic, and Ellie wondered where, *where*, they'd come from.

The one the children liked best contained frog onomatopoeia. They counted five and seven syllables by placing their hands under their chins.

After recess, they wrote their own haikus. Ellie circuited the room while their pencils marked their notebooks. Their little hands smoothed away eraser bits back and forth over the page, in a way that resembled ASMR.

One girl wrote a haiku about rainbows, with hearts sketched in the margins, and gave it to Ellie. When Ellie came home, she posted it to the fridge, under a magnet of seashells.

Phoenix saw it and smirked. *"Really?"*

"Don't make fun of it." She shook her head. "No."

"Why not? Remember when I used to come into Viceroy and leave haikus for you on napkins?"

"Why bring up Viceroy?"

"Why not?"

"I don't care actually, you can bring it up. It doesn't really matter."

Awake at night— / the sound of the water jar / cracking in the cold. Why did she have haikus in her head now? She wanted them to stop. Haikus only made her sad. They made her feel something. She asked Phoenix if he wanted mayonnaise on his sandwich. She focused on mayonnaise.

Outside, an ambulance neared their house with its siren. She listened to it approach, then fade into another neighborhood. They sat down to eat in front of the TV, the local news, and the weatherman with the forecast. A cloud, frowning, with rain and snow slanted over its face. Phoenix moved the car, and charged the flashlight batteries.

In the morning, snow covered the ground like a thin blanket with holes in it, ready to come apart. School was closed, but Phoenix had to work.

Through the kitchen window, in the unforgiving light of morning, she watched him scrape the windshield. She looked at the trees, their white limbs. Birds disappeared over the roof.

Gray light filled the kitchen, and the kitchen window, and the road outside the window, iced like the surface of a rink. A row of boxwood in the opposite yard stared back at her with their white tips.

It all pierced her. It was beautiful, she thought, but what do you *do* with it? It seemed as though it wasn't enough just to look at beauty—you had to *do* something about it—as though you had to destroy it to be satisfied.

She stroked the cat, and felt the static electricity down

his back. She swept the floor, cornering a spider with the broom, and raised her boot. Then she changed her mind. She crouched beside it. She watched it play dead.

She turned the TV to a soap opera where a woman threatened to destroy another woman. She heard a haiku in her head, like an itch, where reason should be. There was a time when she would have gone to the bar, but there was nothing to find there, she knew that now. She picked at a mole on her side, near the band of her bra.

She looked at screen-life. Image, image, image. Swipe, delete, like. She decided to organize the pictures Phoenix had printed at Walgreens.

Like, like, like.

He worried the pictures on his phone would somehow erase and lose themselves in the cloud, so he printed them at Walgreens and brought them home in their paper envelope.

She put one in a frame—Ellie and Phoenix, the versions of themselves they wished to present to the camera—on a rock just outside the entrance to Wilson Park. As she pressed the image into the glass, her fingerprints made smudge marks that looked like great gray clouds, hanging just over their heads.

She burned the thighs of her jeans dragging the space heater from room to room. In some moments, the orange glow of the on-hot button seemed comforting; in others, it announced itself like an alarm.

She waited all afternoon for Phoenix to come home. But when his car pulled up, and the front door opened, she was disappointed. She wanted to talk. About everything, about nothing. But that was unfair—how could he walk through the door and be a different person?

"What do you want to do for dinner?" he asked, turning on the TV.

"I'm not really hungry."

"How is that?"

"I'm not that hungry these days. I graze."

His phone rang. "It's my mom," he said. He answered, then went into the bedroom, closing the door behind him. He never talked to his mother on the phone in front of Ellie. They were in constant communication, those two, which was stunning to someone who talked to her parents only every few months.

What did they talk about? His mother didn't like Ellie, but Ellie didn't take it personally.

When he cruised back into the living room a half hour later, Ellie was lying on the sofa. He looked at her. His eyes moved to her back. "Are you *bleeding*?" he asked.

She twisted around slowly with reserve energy, to see the blood on her white shirt. "Oh. I removed a mole this morning," she explained.

"You did what?" He went to her.

"Yeah. I removed a mole by myself," she said.

She showed him her back; he turned away in revulsion.

"Ellie, what the fuck. Why?"

"I don't know. It seemed interesting at the time."

"Interesting? What—you used a razor? Let's put something on it."

She followed him into the bathroom.

"Have you had a text about school tomorrow? It's supposed to be nine degrees tonight. Everything's going to freeze."

"It's canceled."

He put his arm around her. "I'd come get you for lunch, or something, but I have a meeting." Then he said: "Maybe—if you want company, well, I wish you'd call my mom. I know she likes you . . ."

They watched the screen.

"What are you thinking?" he said.

"What? Nothing. Just blank."

"No, really, tell me. What are you thinking?"

"I mean—nothing. Sometimes hi, how was your day, is enough."

"Well—it seemed like you wanted to talk earlier." He shook his head. "I don't get you sometimes."

She slept late. When she woke, Phoenix had already left for work, and the room was turned on with the sun. Outside, the world was stained in bright colors, turning slush to snow on the wet road. Her eyes hurt. When a car rushed by, its tires slashed through the weather like the sound of something being ripped open.

She rearranged the chairs in the living room. She alphabetized the games on the shelf, and dusted the kitsch on the mantle from Phoenix's mother: HARMONY sitting in silver metal letters, painted seashells, LIVE LAUGH LOVE etched into a picture frame with a picture of Phoenix as a baby.

She looked at the room in various angles, thinking about Rachel. She wanted to call her. She wanted to collapse in bed with her somewhere and tell her everything. She knew pieces about her—tennis, a tennis-pro boyfriend. This was Fayetteville, after all; everyone knew something. She knew that Chloe and Jim lived together.

And that was all right.

There were so many things she wanted to tell Rachel about the Montessori children. She wanted to do their voices. Last week, the real teacher told the class that orcas and dolphins, along with humans and monkeys, were among the only species who could recognize their reflection in a mirror. A boy raised his hand and, very serious, asked, "But how do you get an orca in front of a mirror?"

But Ellie didn't call her.

Saturday afternoon was cold and clear. She waited for the minutes between day and night to close into each other, and the stars to turn on, before she worked the hook and eye of her green dress into place. She smoothed out the long sleeves and pinned a barrette with a single pearl in her hair.

She tried not to think about Michael, about the last time she wore this dress: *Turn around.* She kept reminding herself that he might not be there, not to get worked up, not to drink—at least not Jameson. Part of her knew she would, and it made her sad knowing she couldn't trust herself.

Phoenix took selfies for his mom, who responded with exclamation points and emojis. Then Ellie buttoned her coat and slid her hands into gloves, and they walked up the hill holding hands. The party was at the convention center a few blocks away—a ten-minute walk.

She felt in control, like nothing could throw her without her permission. Phoenix talked excitedly about work and she forgot to listen. So it was all very regular and safe.

They walked up the steps, the huge gray slabs, to the convention center. The front of the building returned her image. She looked at it without feeling, then opened the door, and watched her body disappear into it.

A jazz trio played. The room was huge, with fluorescent lights and white tablecloths that made circles all over the room, the knives gleaming.

Phoenix picked up their number, and she followed him to the table. She sat next to him, stiff as a drink, napkin in her lap. She needed a drink. She shouldn't have one. Phoenix talked to his boss, and his boss's partner. They were introduced. "What do you want to drink?" Phoenix asked. "I'm going to get something."

She shouldn't have one. "Jameson," she said. "Just neat."

Then she saw him. Sitting across the room. In a cloud of other people who were not Michael, their only distinction this fact. Her eyes stayed on him as he laughed easily, though she could tell, even from here, that he was using his fake laugh. Surrounded by husbands and wives and partners, he seemed alone. She scanned the room. After a while, she felt it, she became certain: no Marianne. This, she hadn't prepared for. She thought both would come, or neither would come. She felt a disturbing kind of hope rise through her chest.

She stared at him until, eventually, under the weight of her gaze, he looked back and smiled uneasily, amused. He turned away and scanned the room, but his eyes came back to her with the secret knowledge of their history.

"I'm having a good time," she said, into Phoenix's ear. Phoenix looked at her and smiled, squeezing her leg—the point—so Michael could see her intimacy with someone else. She felt Michael watching her. She looked back at him. This time they held each other's gaze.

After the speeches and tiramisu, and the coffee with its silver cups of cream, she went to the bathroom down the hallway. Outside the door, Michael was waiting.

"Fancy seeing you here," he whispered.

She held her breath. "Hello." She was still drying her hands, flicking off beads of water. Jameson stroked her head and her heart. She smiled.

"What are you doing with that guy," he said.

She almost laughed. "How can you ask me that?"

"I miss you."

She shook her head. "Stop, no."

"I mean it."

She glanced behind her. Nobody could see them now, but she was aware that anyone could turn the corner. "Why don't you get Marianne to come to my house and tell me so in person."

"Don't do that."

She smiled. "Do what?"

"Ellie, I had no choice. You know I had no choice. You know I didn't mean any of it . . . She made me."

She rolled her eyes.

Oh god—she'd been so good for months. For *months* she hadn't cried. For months she'd been calm, she'd been in control. Then it snowed, and now Michael says three things to her, and now all that didn't count anymore. He was undoing her, right before her eyes.

She heard footsteps and turned around.

Phoenix's boss's partner nodded to them absently, then went inside the men's room. She started to walk away.

"Hey—" Michael whispered.

She turned around.

He paused. "I like your dress."

People migrated to the bar, at last. Michael stood within earshot, with enough room to feel out of reach from her and Phoenix, who was talking excitedly to somebody about a start-up, something or other.

"Are you happy," Michael said, without looking at her.

His voice matched the pitch of the noise around them.

"Yeah," she said. "I am."

"Really?"

"Yes, I am."

"I don't believe you."

She glanced at him sideways. "Well, I am."

"Marianne and I are separated," he said.

"Oh, hey," Phoenix said, wanting to introduce Ellie to his new friend, a woman wearing bright lipstick and a skinny black tie. Michael stepped out of the way, and moved through the crowd, closer toward the bar. They talked for a while about apps, but Ellie kept one eye on Michael.

"Are you ready?" Phoenix asked Ellie. "It's getting late, we should go, yeah?"

Ellie nodded, but her legs stayed in place. She felt put on pause while the room spun. She watched Michael order another drink, and she wanted one, too. "I'll get our coats," Phoenix said, touching her shoulder.

The air was crisp like money, the stars pinned so sharply to the sky that you could cut the night with scissors. Even the dead tree limbs, even the street signs and parked cars hummed with life. She stopped and stood in a pitch of lamplight, its hard white energy. "I forgot my gloves," she announced.

Phoenix took two more steps, stopped, then rolled his head back. "Really? No . . ."

"I'm going back to get them."

"We'll get them tomorrow." His eyes shone with wine. "I promise, we'll go back tomorrow."

"No, I need them."

"Why? They're just—gloves."

"I need them."

"Okay." He shrugged and sighed loudly. "Let's go back, then."

"We don't *both* need to go. I'll just run. I'll go really fast. I'll just run and get them."

He stood there. Was he going to wait for her?

"It's freezing," she added. "I'll see you back at the house, okay?"

The confusion in his silence pained her.

"Okay?" she repeated.

"I'm not going to just leave you."

She nodded; she forced a smile, hating herself. "Just go," she said. When he protested, she cut him off with, "I'll see you back at home. Really." She turned and began walking.

She walked and didn't turn around. She didn't want to see him standing there; she had to lock out the shame. She silenced her phone. He called out to her once, but she kept walking. She pushed open the glass doors of the hotel, nearly breathless. Artificial heat stung her forehead. She walked through the lobby without meeting anyone's eye, and regarded the empty spaces around the bar.

Then she saw him.

She looked away before their eyes could meet. She sat next to an older man in a blue suit, whose light blue eyes stayed in the bar mirror, fixed into space. She smiled at the bartender. "Hey. Did you find a pair of gloves?"

He looked briefly behind the counter, then shook his head—no time for gloves, it seemed.

Anyway, she knew her gloves were folded neatly in her purse. She touched them. "Oh well," she said. "I'll have a Jameson, I guess, since I'm here."

When the seat beside her opened, Michael took it. Their knees touched. He took her wrist, then looked around and placed a hand on her knee. "You're back."

She threw her Jameson back, then felt it spread through her body. "I cannot *believe* how you hurt me, Michael."

"Oh, baby," he sighed.

She ordered another one.

"Ellie, I had to try to make my marriage work. I *had* to. But we're not together anymore."

"You're getting divorced?"

"We're separated."

"But not divorced."

"What's the difference? We're not together."

She thought there was a difference.

"Just—we thought we had problems before? Throw a baby in there. It's murder. Marianne. She's gone completely insane."

"Well," Ellie said, making a show of being fair. "I guess it is hard being a new mother."

"Oh, sure, being a mother is the hardest job in the world. Just ask a coal miner."

"Is she happy being a mother?"

"Who knows." He shook his head. "No, she loves Stella. She's a good mother. She gives her everything, and I give Marianne everything—that's what I don't—" He stopped himself. "I mean, she's got money, she doesn't work, she plays tennis all day, she hangs around with this aging—look, I don't want to talk about Marianne."

Her heart pounded through her dress. She touched her drink, then his hand. "What else," she said.

He took his hand away. "We can't talk here like this, in front of—I mean, I can't give Marianne any reasons to be suspicious."

"Why? You're separated."

"She hates you. She's looking for all and any reasons to take Stella away from me. Come see me tomorrow."

"Where are you staying?"

"The El."

"The *El* . . . naturally."

"I'm predictable, what can I say?" He put his hand on her knee briefly, then caught himself. "Tomorrow. Come to me—we can talk about it. Just come, okay? One o'clock?"

"Okay," she said. "I'll see you."

Cold air rushed to her head like a brain freeze. She nearly laughed. She breathed. What was she *doing*? She didn't care, because she was so happy.

Wind blew across her as she practically jogged down the sidewalk, thinking her Michael-thoughts. She thought about him as she crossed the street and touched her gloves inside her purse. She thought about him even as she rehearsed lies in her head for Phoenix.

She walked down the sidewalk, slower now, toward home, and thought about Michael. Michael, Michael, Michael. An animal rustled at the back of a trash can rolled to the curb. She felt an animal inside her, wanting to get out. Wind blew her hair around one shoulder. She felt her hair trying to leave her body.

The train went by.

When she tiptoed into bed, she knew from Phoenix's breathing that he was awake, turned from her, pretending to be asleep. She lay awake, staring at the ceiling, rehearsing lies: The bartender returned her gloves, then she ended up having another drink—that was no crime, was it?

She woke up without a hangover. The bands of pressure around her body were not there, she realized, because she was still drunk. Life was wonderful, oh, why, *why* had she ever decided to forget Jameson? Why wasn't she always at least *slightly* intoxicated? The world and everything in it was so much clearer.

She posed behind Phoenix in the bathroom mirror. He went on brushing his teeth as if he couldn't feel her presence. She put her arms around him and kissed his back, which was a little repulsive, but what the hell. "Let's have mimosas," she suggested.

He spit. "Okay." But he didn't look at her.

She tried to joke with him—she was so happy—but he kept a frosty distance all morning, even as they drank from tall skinny glasses and listened to *Wait Wait . . . Don't Tell Me!* at the island in the kitchen.

He said his friends were coming over.

That was all right. That would make it easy to escape this afternoon. She kept tapping her foot against her chair leg, as she worked both crosswords in the online paper, the easy and the hard, while Phoenix played *Angry Birds*.

"I didn't know you were going back to school," she told him.

He was barely sipping his mimosa, but she had already drained her glass and refilled it twice. "What?" he asked.

"Nursing school," she replied.

"Oh." He looked at his full glass and smiled a little. He drank. "All right."

His friends smoked from the vaporizer and played *League* something—*League of Legend*. Something about warfare, she thought. They consoled Dane, whose girlfriend had kicked him out. Now he was homeless and needed somewhere to stay while he got his new band going. Ellie worried Phoenix would offer him their second bedroom.

On second thought, that was all right. Michael was back; maybe she wouldn't be living here much longer.

Ellie listened to them through the cracked door of the bedroom as she took a shower and stepped into clothes.

The girl was superficial, they told Dane. She worked at *Dillard's*. She was a spoiled, materialistic bitch, who thought she was a queen. "Women are holes," Phoenix said.

That surprised her. Oh well, she thought, braiding her hair and wrapping the black band around her split ends.

She changed her shirt.

Phoenix walked in as she worked the last button and said, "Why are you in such a good mood?"

"I'm not," she said.

"Mom's birthday is next week. I want us to do something special."

Why? Ellie thought. *She's just a hole.*

"Thinking early dinner at the café," he said, daring her to disagree.

"All right," she said, smiling.

His tone softened. "Really?"

"Of course," she said, believing next week, even tomorrow, would never come. The only thing that existed was this afternoon. "Hey, I'm going to the library."

"Now?"

"I want to check out this book of haikus." It was true— she did *want* to, but the library had weird weekend hours.

• • •

She walked through campus toward the El, past the tall brick buildings standing in their places like actors, all dead on a Sunday. Bare trees lined the sidewalk with its scroll of names—everyone who had ever graduated—announcing themselves as she walked over them. *Jackson Thomas Shaw.* Here was the class of 1918, 1919. *Evelyn Grace Shopoff.*

She looked back and saw them here, these people. Then she looked back and saw Rachel on the lawn, walking through a game of Frisbee golf in her boots and black leggings, JanSport hanging off one shoulder. She pictured Rachel in the doorway now, about to swing open the door.

Ellie took a seat on a black bench that faced the El. She texted Michael that she was outside. She looked up and wondered which room was his, which Juliet balcony, which window with its strip of curtain against the pane? She rubbed the smooth face of her phone with her thumbs.

She looked at her phone.

Several minutes passed.

The mimosas began to weigh drowsily on her, as if the alcohol could take her down by the shoulders, as if she could turn to liquid and evaporate on this bench.

She looked at her phone.

She stared at the dark windows of the El. Birds flew from the tree above her. She looked at her phone again.

Nothing.

Church bells rang across the street. A haiku ran through her head the way a score scrolls across a sports channel: *Coolness / the sounds of the bell / as it leaves the bell.*

Finally her phone blinked with a text. Michael. He was in the car, he said. Traffic. She stared at the letters on the screen, which jumbled together. They cleared into words, then jumbled again. The outline of Michael's daughter appeared in his words. Michael has a daughter, she said to herself.

He wrote: *Soon.*

When she didn't write back, he wrote again, telling her not to go anywhere.

Nobody just disappears, he'd said in the sticky booth of Que Sera.

She started to respond, then erased the message slowly, letter by letter. Finally, she typed that she had to go.

Don't go yet.

She didn't move for several moments, waiting for—what?

Her phone blinked again. She took a breath and read his words: *I love you. Don't forget it.*

She erased it so she wouldn't cry. She stood up and started walking, trying not to think, but thinking anyway, that people *did* disappear.

She stared at the names in the sidewalk, the people she walked over. Don't think, she told herself. Don't think. *Evelyn Grace Shopoff* would never turn back into the now-dead Evelyn Grace Shopoff.

How long could she go like this?

She walked.

She walked past the El, in the opposite direction of Diane Lane, past Driscoll Hall and a fraternity house with its letters slanted on the roof, streamers leftover from a party. She wasn't sure where she was going.

She walked up the street to the bars lined beside each other like contestants in a beauty contest. She thought of the people in high-backed booths about to leave, and those who would stay all night. She walked past Condom Sense, the sex shop, with its rainbow letters on the window beside the bookstore with children's books propped in the window.

Brunch was going on in the café. The laughter of mimosa-drinkers reached her through the open window as she walked under the restaurant balcony.

She passed the closed liquor store, and the convenience store with its electrical wires twisted in front, and the patio bar near the intersection, where the BioLife crowd drank on Sundays after donating plasma. The marquee advertised three-dollar Bloody Marias all day until seven. She didn't recognize anyone standing on the patio, smoking cigarettes. As she walked past, a man called out, "Where you going, girl?"

She turned around without thinking, but she couldn't untangle the voice from the crowd. She smiled out of nervous habit, and kept walking. Wind blew through the holes in her jeans. She kept going.

"Hey, girl," someone yelled.

She kept walking.

"Where are you going?"

ACKNOWLEDGMENTS

would like to thank the following people for their help with this book, all in different ways: my amazing agent Henry Dunow, Dave Lucas, Rolph Blythe, Megan Fishmann, and Pam and Warren Seay.

Thanks especially to Skip Hays, for educating me, and for the conversation of nine years.

I'm also grateful to the Vermont Studio Center and the Kimmel Harding Nelson Center for the Arts for time and space.